The Cornfields of Coaley Creek

Denvil Mullins

The Overmountain Press

JOHNSON CITY, TENNESSEE

ISBN 1-57072-011-8

2 3 4 5 6 7 8 9 0

This book is dedicated to my brothers and sisters,
and to the memory of my dear father, mother, and brother Kitty.

All of the characters' names in *The Cornfields of Coaley Creek* are fictitious, the work of the author's imagination. If I have used anyone's real name in my book, it was coincidental.

Introduction

In this book of short stories, my intention is to bring back to life those happy, humorous years when the Cornfield family worked and laughed its way through an era that time has almost forgotten: the era of the large family. During that past, so long ago it seems, a man wasn't a man if he didn't have about a dozen strong, healthy children to help him to subsist, and a strong, healthy wife to bear those little ankle-biters who grew up to be his helpers.

The typical Appalachian family is brought out in this book—a family with a lot of pride. So many people speak of the hard times of the past. Times are usually as hard as one makes them, or permits them to be. If a person has a little grunt and growl in him, he can stay a step ahead of hard times. He can't look back, though, because it might step in his tracks just as fast as he steps out of them, and if he tarries just a little, hard times might overtake him.

The Cornfields were of that surviving, laughing, fun-loving breed; they seemed to work to live and live to work, scratching in every place that looked fruitful, working for a living instead of looking for a handout.

When I last visited Coaley Creek, the steep slopes of the little hillside farms that once groaned under the heavy loads of growing crops had become an expanse of level ground. The coal company which bought that land so long ago had stripped it of its coal deposits, leaving the land permanently scarred.

As I walked over the leveled earth which was once Marn's and Vann's hillside farm, in my mind I could still see the little boxed house with its wide cracks covered with weather strips to block out the cold winter winds. I heard the echoes of that happy, laughing family of eleven children, and of riding wooden-wheeled wagons down Grandpa's pasture field. I heard Judge L. scream once more as he grabbed the wheels with his hands, trying to stop the moving wagon. I heard so clearly Bart's laughter after having played that prank on Judge L. The echo of the splashing in the old swimming hole brought back fond memories of a time long past.

If doctors, scientists, and researchers could bottle laughter or make it into a pill and then prescribe it to depressed people, the medical profession could advance its research by centuries. Laughter can never hurt anyone; it can only help. It takes a far greater effort to frown and cry than it does to grin all over one's self.

Without the modern conveniences like those we have today, to keep them glued to a screen and plastered to a couch, the Cornfield children learned to be craftsmen. They made their own toys to play with, preparing themselves for a future in an ever-changing world.

The big family has scattered over this great country. Each year, though, they meet somewhere to spend a weekend together, where they reminisce and relive those memorable days of long ago—days that will never come back—days which the family can only return to in memory.

I hope the reader enjoys the humor of this book and can in some way relate to the many monkeyshines that kept the Cornfields happy as they dug in the mines for coal and tilled the steep fields in their efforts to make an honest living.

I hope the elders who read this book can reminisce as I have while writing it, and the younger generations can explore a time much different from theirs.

Table of Contents

Glossary

bait—a huge meal

bale-hay wire—hay baling wire

bee smoker—a beekeeper's apparatus for making smoke and forcing it into a hive to stupefy the bees so the honey can be removed

cant hook—a lever with a movable hook at one end, used to grip and turn over logs

chop sack—a sack or bag for packaging hog feed

dewclaw—a functionless inner claw or toe in some dogs, not reaching the ground in walking

dog hole—coal mine

double-shovel plow—a plow with two points for cultivating corn

drift mouth—entrance to a coal mine

fer-field—far field; a field at the farthest distance from the farmhouse

gnyamming—viewing food noisily with the mouth open

gons—gondolas; railroad cars for hauling coal or ballast

goober—peanut

granny knot—a knot differing from a square knot in having the ends crossed the wrong way

griller—gorilla

headmark—bonus point earned while doing schoolwork

hog-dollar—silver dollar

hog's rooter—hog's snout; hog's nose

hope him—helped him

idee—idea

jarsh—to scrape a vegetable—usually a potato—to a mushy pulp

jiffy—short time; moment

'lectric—electricity

'lexeycuted—electrocuted

marvel—marble

mast—acorns, chestnuts, beechnuts, hickory nuts, etc. on the ground

milk gap—a place in a fence, usually in a corner, to milk cows

monkeyshine—a mischievous trick

'nanner—banana

noggin—a person's head

pl'ike—play like

poke—a paper bag

possumin'—playing possum
riffles—ripples in a river
scrouge—room, space
shoat—a young weaned pig
spacial—special
stack cake—a cake made with several layers, with spiced apples between the
    layers; a molasses cake
tater—potato
taw—an especially fine shooting marble
yarn—a wild, unbelievable story
zillion—a very large, indefinite number

Dump's Magic Bottle

Late one summer afternoon, Uncle Fate Cornfield walked up the lane toward his brother's house on Coaley Creek. There was something odd about Fate's stride. It was stable. Ordinarily, the man walked with a little stagger-stumbling gate—not that afternoon, though. He was walking just as straight as any other Coaley Creek gentleman. Usually the Coaley Creek gentlemen had that stagger-stumbling gait due to some nervous disorder—usually caused by the gentlemen's consumption of too much corn liquor.

'Shine and home brew were the main stimulating drinks on Coaley Creek. Moonshine was the most popular. Home brew came in at a very close second. Anyone could concoct that drink—just throw together anything that would ferment and you could have a good drink—so they say.

Fate Cornfield would not have anything to do with cheap home brew. "Give me 'shine. Don't insult me by making an offer of anything that ain't worth snot," he always told anyone who offered him a drink. "If you don't have any good 'shine to offer, don't offer me anything at all."

"Here comes Fate," Vann Cornfield called out to Marn as she emerged from the kitchen.

Marn sat in a straight-back chair in the front bedroom. There was no fire in the grate, but from force of habit Marn sat resting in front of the fireplace.

Vann watched Fate walk toward the house by way of the lane formed by a rail fence on each side of the narrow wagon road—the access route to the Cornfield Estate, if one could call a three-room house and a few acres stuck in the hillside an estate.

"Does Fate look like he's walking all right, Vann?" Marn asked. "You know that he has rheumatiz and can't walk very straight. Sometimes he has the blind-staggers and the wobbly-limps when his hips and knees hurt real bad and give way on him."

"The only thing that gives way on Fate Cornfield is his weakness to suck the end of that ol' liquor bottle that he carries around all the time," Vann snapped.

"Yeah, he gets a little tipsy before he leaves home with his bottle," Marn laughed. "Then he compares tastes with his drinking buddies 'long the road as he makes his way from place to place, and it takes a lot of drinks to give him a taste. He's pretty smart, ol' Fate is." Marn chuckled as he thought about his brother's enjoyment of swapping drinks with his friends.

"A drunk ain't smart," Vann replied, pondering what her husband had said. "The only thing that a drunk can do that's smart is to quit his drinking, and Fate ain't ready to do anything that smart."

"He'll quit one of these days, and then we can laugh about his past conduct," Marn chuckled.

"It'll have to be a lot funnier than it is right now before you'll get a laugh out of me," Vann stated emphatically.

"Hon, someday you'll look back and laugh about what Fate does," Marn said to his wife, chuckling at her fussing.

"I'm afraid he'll fall over dead along the road somewhere before I have a chance to laugh," Vann snapped, continuing to watch the approach of her brother-in-law.

Vann Cornfield was a saint of a woman. She had been raised in a family where moonshine was a part of her everyday life. She did not condone, nor did she disapprove of, the making of moonshine. Her father, Dalker Skinner, made his living on the five hundred-acre farm, where the major crop was corn. Part of the corn crop was made into liquor—rotgut whisky—for personal use, and for sale, of course.

Vann had accepted the fact that her father had to make a living somehow, but she did not accept the actual act of moonshining as being a lily-white vocation. There had always been a roof over her head, clothes on her back, and food on the table. As long as the money was used in that manner, she figured everything was all right.

"Fate's marching as straight as a fishing pole," Vann noticed. She stood in front of the window, her hands resting on her hips. "I hope he don't have anything to drink with him," she said in a low voice, almost a whisper, speaking quietly to herself.

"What was that you said, Hon?" Marn asked, rising from his chair. He walked over and joined his wife at the window. "'Pon my word and honor, I think he's as sober and clean as a Virginia gentleman!" he exclaimed.

"Right now he is, but wait till he gets in the house. Then we'll see just how long he can keep hisself clean and sober," Vann quipped, turning and walking away from the window.

"Hey! He's got Ol' Drum with him!" Marn exclaimed excitedly. "We'll be going fox huntin' this evening. He'll stay sober tonight, for sure. Fate knows that I won't put up with drinkin' while we're fox huntin'."

"He's a bad influence on you, and with our boys growing up, I don't want that ol' liquor around them," Vann said, leaving the front room and going to the kitchen to prepare a snack, which was a natural reaction when there was company at her house.

"You don't think that your dad and brothers are an influence on me and the boys, do you?" Marn said, smiling.

"Not like your brother," Vann called from the kitchen, where she was in the process of kindling a fire in the wood-burning range.

"Hon, your dad and brothers make enough of that stuff to float a battleship up Coaley Creek. They keep it in and around the house and in ever' building and groundhog hole on his farm," Marn said. "You know that I have access to ever' bottle on the place. The boys have probably sampled it and know what it is. Do you say that ain't an influence on me? If you don't think so, then they must have changed the meaning of 'influence' since I quit school. I guess they changed it to mean my brother. Vann, Hon, you look over your family's faults and make excuses for them and then complain about Fate's shortcomin's."

"My paw and my brothers don't bring it in here in front of the young 'uns," Vann replied, continuing her chore of kindling a fire.

"No, 'cause the young 'uns can go to his house and see it, which must make it all right," Marn argued. "I'm sure that Fate won't bring a bottle in the house this time." Marn smiled as his brother took a bottle from his pocket and hid it in a hollow log in the barn wall. "Don't worry about Fate, Hon."

"I don't worry about Fate," Vann returned. "I worry about you and our young 'uns." She slammed the stove lid down, signifying her disgust at the thought of having someone drinking around her children.

Fate chained Ol' Drum to a front porch post, patted the hound gently on the head, then entered the farmhouse without knocking on the door to announce his arrival.

* * * *

Bart and Jake were riding out trees in the wooded area behind the barn.

Dump sat on a pile of hay in the barn loft, relaxing. He heard a tree fall in the thicket behind the barn, accompanied by a shrieking scream. Jake was in the top of that tree, getting ready to ride it out, when Bart began wielding his axe on the three-inch trunk.

Each time Jake climbed a sapling to ride it out, Bart chopped it down, just to see Jake fall. Bart enjoyed the sound of the shrill screams of his younger brother plummeting to earth with a felled tree.

"You're crazy, Bart," Jake yelled, striking the ground with a thump. "I thought you was gonna put that axe back at the chop block."

"I was gonna do it as I said I would, but I couldn't resist chopping down another tree," Bart said, laughing. "I'll put it away right now." He walked toward the woodyard situated between the barn and the house.

Jake found another tree to ride out, and since Bart was no longer around as a menace to his health, he began to climb. As he reached the top of the limber hickory sapling, he heard an axe strike the tree and felt the vibration.

Bart chopped as fast as he could, grinning with glee.

"Bart, you hateful thing!" Jake screamed, sliding down the tree to escape the fall. He was a little too late, though. The tree struck the ground with a thud, and so did Jake.

Bart laughed hilariously as Jake rose to a sitting position and looked around, a stunned expression on his face.

Dump heard all that went on, since he was so close to the arena of action. He knew very well that his younger siblings could get hurt if he didn't intervene in the goings on. He rose from his seat on the soft hay and descended the ladder to the ground. A big smile split his face. "I'll have me some good fun out of them two," he said out loud. He had seen Uncle Fate hide the liquor bottle in the barn wall.

"Would you fellers like to have some excitement?" Dump asked, approaching the playing boys.

"We're having all the excitement we can stand right now," Bart said, then began to chop a tree that Jake had just scaled.

"You may be having fun, Bart, but I ain't when I hit the ground so hard," Jake cried. "Now stop that!" His scream was accompanied by the whooshing of the falling tree.

"You're having fun, too. You may not know it, but you are," Bart said as Jake hit the ground. "Go ahead and admit it now."

"That could stunt my growth, Bart," Jake groaned. "I'm just a tad woozy."

"I've got something that will make you forget about stuntin' your growth and feeling woozy," Dump told Jake. "What I have will make you feel real good and about ten foot tall to boot."

"Let me have it, Brother," Jake said, rising from the ground where he had landed with the falling tree. He staggered a step or two, pretending to be dizzy.

"You'll have to promise not to tell anyone," Dump warned. "This is to be our secret—ours and ours only. Do you boys promise?"

"Cross my heart and hope that you die, Dump," Bart promised.

"Hope that I die?" Dump said. "Make your own promise with hope that you die 'stead of me being the one snuffed out with your wish."

"I was just joshing you," Bart laughed. "I don't want nary one of us to kick out. Come on and show us what you've got," he coaxed.

With their curiosity raised, Bart and Jake crowded close to Dump, giving him a chance to whisper his confidence if he wished to.

"Back up and give me some scrouge, boys. I don't have to whisper since no one's around to hear us," Dump said, elbowing his brothers away. "Do you know that Uncle Fate come to visit awhile ago?"

"No, I didn't know that," Bart said, looking toward the house, hoping to see his favorite uncle. "I like Uncle Fate and I'm going to see him."

"No, don't go right now," Dump said, grasping Bart by the shoulder, slowing his effort to make a dash for the house. "Don't you want to hear my secret?"

Dump was in the process of revealing his confidence when his father and his Uncle Fate emerged from the house.

The two men were dressed in their hunting clothes. Each wore a miner's cloth hat with a carbide light held in place in the slot of the leather lamp holder.

Old Drum charged at his chain, causing Old Bowser to come out of his kennel, barking and charging at his chain.

"Ort to be a good hunt. The dogs are really excited," Uncle Fate avowed.

"We'll have a fox up and running in no time at all," Marn predicted, unsnapping Old Bowser's chain.

"Don't say anything to them about our secret," Dump warned the two younger boys as they ran excitedly to greet their uncle.

"We won't," Bart promised, running at breakneck speed toward the hunters.

"We won't," Jake said, echoing Bart's assurance.

"Howdy, boys," Uncle Fate spoke, greeting the lads.

"Howdy, Uncle Fate," Bart spoke, grinning up at his favorite uncle, squinting an eye against the sun at Fate's back.

Jake echoed with "Hello, Uncle Fate."

"How're you boys doing?" Uncle Fate asked, patting Bart on the head. He tousled the boy's unruly hair.

"Okay," the brothers replied simultaneously.

"Dump's going to tell me and Bart a secret," Jake blurted out, looking up at Uncle Fate.

"He is?" Uncle Fate smiled. "You know that if he tells you, it won't be a secret any longer. I believe he ort to keep his secret to hisself. I'm afraid that you might tell it to somebody else if he tells you."

"What good's a secret if you can't tell it to else folks?" Jake asked.

"Well, I guess you have a point there," Uncle Fate laughed, pulling Jake's black hair. "I bet your nickname's 'Whitey.'"

"No!" Jake responded. "Don't you know black hair when you see it, Uncle Fate?"

"Don't guess I do," Uncle Fate laughed loudly, slapping his legs animately.

Uncle Fate enjoyed a good joke and a laugh, and the boys could expect to be teased when their favorite uncle came for a visit.

Marn and Uncle Fate put the lead chains in their knapsacks with their blankets.

The blankets were for a good nap by the fire while the hunters waited for the dogs to chase the fox back into hearing range after a long circuit through the mountains. A red fox will often run for miles in its efforts to elude the ensuing hounds.

The two Walker hounds stiff-legged around each other, sniffed at their most conspicuous parts, and scratched the soft earth with their hind feet, throwing dirt up in the air. They hiked a leg and marked a fence post, one after the other, and then raced toward the woods to start their search for a fox to chase.

"Have a good hunt," Dump said as Marn and Uncle Fate followed the dogs toward the woods.

"We will," Uncle Fate stated, rubbing Jake's head once more. "You boys be good and keep out of trouble."

"We'll be sure to do that," Dump told him, a sly smile spreading over his face as he watched the hunters follow the dogs toward the woods.

"You're up to something unusual, Dump, ain't you?" Bart said, turning his attention from the departing hunters back to his older brother.

"No, not up to anything unusual. I can do some exciting magic. I want you two to see me do it," Dump replied.

"What kind of magic?" Jake asked, showing interest in what Dump had said.

"Black magic, I would say," Bart laughed, not believing Dump's revelation.

"Not black magic or white magic, either," Dump told them. "It's just good magic. See my right hand? Now, see my left hand?" He held his hands up to show that they were empty.

"Yeah, you just proved that you have two hands—a left and a right," Bart said. "Jake," he continued, turning to the youngster, "Dump has two hands. That's great magic, ain't it?"

"Yeah, it sure is," Jake giggled.

"Now, Jake, let's me and you do magic," Dump said, holding his hands up. "There's nothing in either hand."

Jake raised his hands, looked at them, and said, "See, Bart, I have two hands, just like Dump."

"No, boys. I only wanted you to see that I don't have anything in my hands," he said, smiling. "Now," he continued, "you see that I don't have anything in my hands. Just stand still and watch."

Dump put his hand into the end of a hollow log in the barn wall. When he removed his hand from the hole in the log, he held a long-necked quart bottle in his tightly-clasped fingers.

"That ain't magic," Bart said, looking at the bottle that Dump held out for him to see. "You put it in that log, didn't you?"

"No, I didn't put it in there. I made some magic," Dump declared, trying to convince the lads that he had really done a magic trick.

"Is that magic supposed to make me feel ten foot tall?" Jake queried, looking at the clear liquid in the bottle. "What's in it, Mister Magic Man?"

"It's clear pop," Dump said, shaking the bottle the way that he had seen his Uncle Fate do.

"Give me a swaller of that pop, Dump," Jake begged.

"Go get me a fruit jar so I can put the pop in it," Dump suggested, pushing Jake toward the smokehouse.

"Why don't we just drink it out of that long-necked bottle?" Bart wanted to know, reaching for it. "I can wrap my mouth around the end of it real easy and guzzle as much as I want at one swig."

"No, we can't do that," Dump said. "We'll pour most of it into a fruit jar, then we'll fill the bottle back full of creek water. I'll do my magic on it and put it back in the log. Next week sometime, we can have another bottle of clear pop. Get me a jar, Jake. I'll pour half of the pop in it, then we'll drink it."

Jake ran to the smokehouse, where Vann kept her empty fruit jars, and quickly returned with a dust-covered quart jar.

Dump emptied most of the liquid from the bottle into the jar without first removing the dust and spiderwebs contaminating the inside. He refilled the bottle with creek water and replaced it in the hollow log. "Jake, you can have the first sup, since you're the littlest," Dump said, handing the glass container to Jake.

Jake slurped a big swallow from the mouth of the jar. His eyes crossed as the air gushed from his wide-opened mouth. He hiccuped a few times, and when he got his breath back, he asked, "What kind of pop is that, Dump? Whew! That stuff would scald a fattenin' hog's rooter off."

"That's hot pop," Dump laughed, reaching for the jar.

Each brother gave the same reaction to his first drink from the jar. The more they drank, the easier it was to swallow and breathe.

"Boy, Dump, I do feel ten foot tall!" Jake said, tiptoeing around after he had had several drinks from the jar. "Give me another swaller, then I'll feel about 'leven foot tall."

As the boys gulped the liquid down their numbed throats, their good feelings turned to dizziness and nausea. By the time the jar was completely empty, all three were puking all over the place.

Dump slowly made his way to the spring that ran from the steep rock cliff behind the house, retching and upchucking almost every step he took. Bart made it to the pig-lot, where he lay in the coolness of a tree's shade. Jake lay in the stuff that the chickens had left as their calling card under the roost in the henhouse. All three boys looked as if they were down for the count.

* * * *

"That's the first time I ever went all the way over to Bass Creek without striking up a fox's trail with these two dogs," Uncle Fate said as he and Marn emerged from the woods, leading the hounds.

"Yeah, it sure is," Marn agreed, stopping to lower the drawbars in the rail fence that encircled the house, farm buildings, and vegetable garden. "We can try it again next week, if you want to."

"Yeah, we'll have to try it again, I guess," Fate said. "Let's stop at the barn, Brother. I've got something wet hid in a holler log in the barn wall. I snuck it in there when I come by this evening."

"I could use a taste of something wet," Marn beamed, speaking so low that it was almost a whisper. "Let's sneak down there and take a snort or two." He still whispered. "I don't want Vann to see me take a drink. We had a little discussion on drinking when she saw you coming up the lane awhile ago."

"She won't see us," Fate said, taking the bottle from the hollow log. He uncorked the bottle and handed it to Marn, giving his brother the first drink, a gesture of his good manners.

Marn took a big swig from the bottle, swallowed loudly, and said, "This stuff's awful weak, Fate. Where'd you get it?"

"Here, let me try it," Uncle Fate said, wiping the neck of the bottle on his shirtsleeve. "I got this from Alphus Bolden. He ain't never let me down before. His product's allus been prime stuff." After several long, gurgling gulps, he smacked his lips together, trying to get all the flavor that he could. "Tastes like branch water to me," he said, spitting on the ground, offering the bottle back to Marn.

"Thanks, but I've had enough," Marn answered, refusing the offer.

"I believe that I've had enough of that stuff, too," Fate said, pouring the remainder of the liquid on the ground. He threw the empty bottle into the thicket behind the barn. "Alf sold me a bad batch that time," he grumbled.

As the brothers walked toward the house, Marn saw Dump sitting on a rock beside the spring, gripping his head with both hands. Drool ran from the boy's open mouth.

"Have you been eatin' green apples, Dump?" Marn wanted to know.

"No, Dad. I wish I had 'stead of what I got a hold of," Dump answered without raising his head.

"That's the answer to the creek water in my bottle," Uncle Fate said, turning to Marn. "He saw me hide it, didn't he?"

"Is that what happened, Dump," Marn asked. "Did you see your uncle hide the bottle in the barn?"

"Yes, Dad," Dump groaned, continuing to hold his head in his shaking hands.

"Did you drink a whole quart?" Marn queried.

"No! Bart and Jake drunk part of it," Dump moaned. "And I'm sure glad they did, too. A whole quart would've killed me deader than an anvil."

"Where's Bart and Jake now?" Marn asked.

"I don't know, Dad," Dump moaned, holding his head, grimacing with the pain shooting through it each time he moved or spoke, and each time Marn spoke to him. He was a miserable person right then.

"I saw Bart in the pig-lot," Clem said as he arrived from his grandfather's house. "Jake's in the henhouse. He must have got tired of gathering eggs and went to sleep. I saw him under the roost. Bart's over in the hog-lot asleep. That's sure a sleepy bunch of boys if you ask me."

Marn and Uncle Fate found Bart and Jake and roused them up to get them to the spring with Dump.

"Dump done magic and found the pop. He give me and Bart some of it," Jake replied, hiccuping loudly. "He put it back in the log to make more pop for next week, but I don't want any more magic pop," he vowed, retching at the thought of another drink of whisky.

"Me neither," Bart said, heaving like a sick dog, remembering the drinking spree.

"I'll take that pop," Clem said excitedly. "I ain't had a good drink of pop in a 'coon's age—not since we went up to Big Onion Gap that time."

"Clem, get out of here and go to the house," Marn ordered.

The dejected boy left the men and went to the house, as ordered.

"Go get them some more of that pop," Marn said, turning to Uncle Fate.

"I think they need another drink. He winked at Fate, indicating that he was only joking.

"No! We don't want nothing else to drink, especially hot pop," Dump said.

Bart and Jake agreed, retching and puking all over the yard.

"Do I look that bad when I get drunk, Marn?" Uncle Fate asked.

"That bad, and worse. You allus want to fight when you get drunk," Marn told him. "Boy, you're a mess when you're tanked up! Worse than these kids by a whole lot."

"I've never seen myself look that bad in my whole life," Uncle Fate said, looking at the three helpless boys.

"That's 'cause you're too drunk to see anything," Marn replied. "Fate, I've had my last drink of liquor. This incident has opened my eyes. Vann was right about whiskey being a bad influence on the boys. Now is as good a time as any for you to mend your ways. Why don't you quit, too?"

"Ain't making no promises, Brother," Fate replied, avoiding eye contact with Marn.

"I believe these three boys will think real hard before they drink magic pop again."

"Amen to that, Dad," Dump groaned.

Jake hiccupped and Bart gagged—their only response.

The Hog Herder

Clem Cornfield was just a youngster when he, his parents, and brothers and sisters moved into their new house on Coaley Creek. He could remember the many good times he had had at the old place that he was leaving. He knew what the new structure looked like, for he and the rest of the family had helped his father construct the building.

Though they were mere lads, Dump, Clem, Bart, Jake, and Judge L. had played a part in the construction of the building, helping their father as much as they could.

Beauty was the eldest of the children. She had helped in the house building in the same capacity as the boys. Girls had to work, too. There was no gender gap or discrimination of any kind on the farm, for the girls had the same opportunity as the boys when it came to helping out with the farm work. The children each got as much work as he or she could stand—more than they really wanted, most of the time.

Marn Cornfield had cleared an area large enough to build a good-sized house.

The house consisted of three bedrooms and a kitchen. Naturally it had a kitchen. A kitchen was certainly a must in a house with a big family. There was no living room at that time. There was no idle time for the family to sit around in a living room doing nothing.

The house had two fireplaces—one in each of two of the bedrooms. Marn and Vann had a fireplace in their room, and there was a fireplace in the room that the smaller children occupied. The cold room, off to the side, had no heating system. That room was for the big boys. They could stand the chill that came through the many cracks formed by the uneven lumber used in the construction of the house. That room was called the cold room because very little heat from the fireplaces reached it due to the draft from the big chimney.

The fireplaces certainly drew well! The old tomcat was afraid to walk across the hearthstone—afraid that it would be sucked up the sooty chimney and carried away to oblivion on a cloud of wood smoke.

Clem could remember how slowly the house had taken shape, from the days of its planning until the day the family moved in.

Marn worked in the coal mines. That one factor slowed construction of the house considerably. He had to stay away from home most of the time, rooming with his cousins in Kentucky, unless someone on Coaley Creek owned a car and worked at the mine with Marn. Then Marn could ride with that person and stay at home. There were times that he had no ride and had to walk eighteen miles, one way, to the mines. Working in the mines was a very hard and trying job, but Marn Cornfield was no slacker. He worked without complaining to provide subsistence for his large, and still growing, family. Often he had to leave home early and return late. That gave him very little time to work on the new house. Weekends found him at the construction site from daylight until dark, and long after dark on many of those days.

The house was finally ready for occupancy, and the family was ready to move in.

"Let's get a move on and try to get most of the house plunder moved to the new house first," Marn ordered his sons as they ran about the yard shouting, laughing, and jumping with joy. "We'll come back this evening, if we have time, and get the rest of the house plunder, can goods, and farm tools. If we ain't able to take it all today, we'll have to come back first thing in the morning. Dump, you're in charge of the horses and wagon," he directed his eldest son. "And, Bart, you're in charge of the cows and calf. Clem can drive the hogs. We'll tie a rope to one of the sow's hind legs. That way you can control her movements a lot better. The six pigs and shoats shouldn't give you any trouble at all. They'll foller right along behind the ol' sow till we get them home."

With Marn and Vann each carrying one of the smaller children and some of the lighter items, the family set out for their new home.

Dump led the wagon train, making the exodus from the little house on the back part of Grandpa Dalker Skinner's farm to the new home, still on Grandpa's farm.

Grandpa gave Vann and Marn some land on which they built the new house. Dalker Skinner owned five hundred acres—more or less—of woodland, swamps, and some fairly good clay-based farmland. He wanted to give his daughter and son-in-law a good start on a fresh plot of ground.

"I'm a pioneer driving a covered wagon across the plains and prairies, headed for California," Dump yelled to be heard above the noise of the squeaking wagon and the jangling of the horses' harness. "Let's get things moving along back there now." He popped an imaginary whip and clucked to his team.

Teed watched the progress of the one-wagon wagon train from his perch on a pile of quilts in the back of the wagon. He could see the hill where his brothers liked to ride wooden-wheeled wagons. He hoped that he and the rest of the brothers could return to ride once more. Surely they could, he reasoned. It was only a quick hop and a slow jump from the new house over in the next hollow.

"I'm on a trail drive from Texas, driving my long-horned cattle up to Montana to start a new ranch in that wild land," Bart pretended, yelling at the two milk cows and one two-month-old calf. He slapped Old Horny on the right flank with a keen sourwood switch, encouraging the patient old cow to move a little faster.

"I'm just an ol' hog herder from up Coaley Creek," Clem sang in a high tenor voice as he followed the grunting sow and squealing piglets.

The sow tried to root in the path in search of something to eat. She found a piece of coal and crunched it with her powerful jaws, while the pigs squealed and ran about, trying to reach a moving teat to nurse a good, sweet, warm meal. The two shoats followed behind the sow and raucous pigs, posing no problem for Clem.

Everyone laughed at Clem's song, and soon the entire family was singing about a hog herder from up Coaley Creek. That helped to pass the time and take their minds off the task that lay ahead.

The trip was simple, but what waited at the end of the trip was on everyone's mind. Unloading the wagon and putting the furniture in its place was the big problem that they were faced with. There were many items to be unloaded and put in piles, in the corners of the rooms and out on the porch, until there was ample time to put them in their permanent places. There were the animals to tend to, to put in makeshift shelters and pens for the night. There was plenty of work to keep everyone busy.

Clem would have to put the sow, pigs, and shoats in a small paling-fence pen, since there were no fences to hold them and keep them from straying into the woods, where they would be hard to find at feeding time. They would have to be let out the next day to roam free and forage on the abundance of mast and herbage beneath the heavy canopy of trees.

A part of the farm had been cleared of trees, leaving a graveyard of dying stumps. The cows could forage for food in that new field. There was an abundance of every kind of food that the animals could want.

* * * *

The trip to the new house was made without mishap. And after a long, hard day of work, the family was tired and hungry. Everyone was ready for something to eat to stoke up his empty energy tank.

Supper consisted of a throw-together of leftovers from previous meals. There had not been ample time to stop to prepare a fresh meal for lunch.

The children were ravenously hungry and showed it by stuffing themselves with the tasty food—almost to the bursting point.

Before bedtime, which would certainly come earlier than the usual chicken-roost time, the boys had a moment to sit around the table and discuss the day's events.

"I surely would like to lead a bunch of settlers across the country," Dump began. "I thought of that while I drove the team and wagon here. I could just imagine myself looking out over my horses' backs at the level land stretching to the far horizon. I would have to dodge prairie dog holes to save my horses, of course, to keep them from breaking their legs. If they did, I'd have to shoot them. I wouldn't want to be out there stranded on the prairie, alone and without horses, water, and food."

"You could catch a wild mustang and tame it and break it to work real quick," Bart said.

"Or you could catch a buffalo and make you a wooden yoke and harness it up to your wagon and make it pull you along," Jake suggested. "Buffalos know how to keep from stepping in prairie dog holes and things like that. They've lived around prairie dogs all of their lives."

"Catching a mustang or a buffalo and breaking them to work would take too long," Dump replied, staring at the wall in deep thought. His mind was out on the plains with a wagon train. "All the good land would be claimed before I could get there. I'd have to be real careful and drive slow in order to dodge the prairie dog holes, rattlesnakes, and stuff like that."

"A rattlesnake couldn't trip a horse. It don't even have legs long enough to trip a big brute like a horse," Clem said, getting into the conversation.

"Rattlesnakes don't have any legs at all," Judge L. said, joining the confab. His sleepy eyes drooped as he tried to concentrate on the conversation. He would have to get in bed pretty soon.

"If they had legs they would just be long lizards," Jake laughed. "Who ever heard of a lizard as long as a rattlesnake?"

"It ain't that the rattlesnakes would trip the horses," Dump said. "A rattlesnake could scare the horses and cause them to bolt and run away. And without control over my horses, they could do real bad damage to their legs, and the wagon, too. With a lot of commotion like that, I could get hurt right along with the horses."

"I read a story one time—it was a dime novel about a trail drive from Texas to Montana," Bart began. "They sure had some rough times on that trail drive. I'd like to drive a big bunch of cattle from one state to another, without all the problems that go with a trail drive. The camping out would be good, though. And the eating would be great, too. I believe I'd get tired of beans all the time, though—for breakfast, dinner, and supper. You know, that's all that people eat in stories about trail drives. Looks to me like there would be more food than just beans all the time. I'd need me some taters, corn bread, meat, and stuff like that once in a while."

"You wouldn't get lost if you eat beans all the time." Dump laughed, thinking of Bart out on the plains, eating beans every meal. "They could find you real easy. They could hear you, and they wouldn't need a bloodhound to sniff you out, either."

"I read in that dime novel where a bunch of cowboys run out of supplies and beans. They had to eat a rattlesnake and a lizard," Bart said, relating more of his story.

"They wouldn't have to eat a snake," Dump said. "Why, they'd have all the meat that they could possibly use. They could kill a cow 'stead of eating a snake. It would take a big pile of rattlesnakes to make one mess to eat. The only part you could eat would be from the extinguisher on back to the rattlers. The rest is just skin, ribs, and guts. Only stupid people would eat a snake when they had a bunch of cows standing around."

"I think snakes have got just a straight gut and a gizzard," Clem said, laughing at his own witticism.

"How was your day, Clem?" Dump asked, changing the subject. "What did you think of and see as you drove the hogs along?"

"I didn't do much thinking," Clem groaned. "All I could see was hogs' rumps, and that didn't give me anything to daydream about."

"Bart," Dump said, laughing at Clem's remark, "you would be a cowboy, driving cattle to Montana. I would be a boss on a wagon train, and Clem would be a hog herder."

Marn had been listening to the lads reminiscing about the day's events. "Well, boys," he began, "it's time to bed down your cows, hobble your horses, and turn in. Tomorrow will probably be a busy day."

Obediently, the boys rose from their resting places at the table and went outside for a brief moment, then retired for the night.

Moving into a strange house did not prevent the family from falling into a deep, restful sleep, causing the building to resound with a symphony of loud snoring.

*   *   *   *

The main problem with moving to the new house was that the length of the nights had changed. They had become so much shorter. Clem thought they had. He mentioned that thought to the rest of the family during breakfast the next morning, and everyone readily agreed with him. There was a bunch of red-eyed people sitting around the breakfast table that morning.

"We have a few more things to haul from the old place today," Marn informed the family. "Clem, I want you to stay here and keep an eye on the cattle and hogs. The cows won't wander far from that fresh grass and stump sprouts. It'll take most of the day to go get the rest of the things and get back. Now, Clem, I want you to keep a watchful eye on the milk and bacon."

"I put you a snack for your dinner in the warming closet of the stove, Clem," Vann reported.

"Now, don't eat it all up as soon as the rest of us leave and then have to go hungry the rest of the day," Dump warned, kidding with Clem.

"If I eat it up real quick, I can jarsh a tater when I get hungry again," Clem said. "I won't go hungry, Dump. I'm smart enough to find something to eat. You can tell by looking at this." Clem patted his stomach.

Clem watched the rest of the family disappear beyond the yellow clay bank over near the milk gap. As they passed from sight beyond the hill, Clem released the hogs and cows from their makeshift quarters to let them drink and graze and forage on the abundance of food. He then lay down on the bed to get some much-needed rest. With such a short night and a lack of rest, he soon drifted off to sleep.

Clem awoke with a start, sat up in the bed, and rubbed the sleep from his eyes. He could not hear anything, causing him to jump out of bed and run to the yard to check on the cows and hogs. Nothing stirred about the place, except for birds and insects—no hogs or cows anywhere. "Don't panic, Clem," he told himself. He had no idea how long he had slept. The stillness became more oppressive. It seemed to close in on the yard and surrounding area from all sides. "Good," he said aloud, seeing the cows grazing contentedly among the stumps in the partially cleared field. "Now, where are the rooters and grunters?" he asked himself, referring to the hogs.

He ran around in a state of panic, searching for the swine. He feared that they had strayed into the woods and would be lost and hard to find. He ran in circles around the house. Finally, in desperation and disgust with himself for losing the hogs, he did the only rational thing that he knew to do. He sat down on a stump and tried to think. He needed to get a handle on the situation. He sat there for only a few minutes, feeling like a dullard, then he heard a grunt and a snort. When he looked around to see where the sound had come from, he saw the sow, pigs, and shoats lying in beds of soft, cool dirt—under the floor of the new house.

Working in the mines had taken up much of Marn's time, and he had not had time to put underpinning around the base of the house to keep out the cold air in winter—and the animals.

After having filled themselves with a big bait of chestnuts, the hogs had sought the coolness of the shade beneath the house.

"I'll take care of this little problem," Clem mumbled to himself. He began a search through the house. He found what he needed and returned, carrying a piece of rope in each hand. He tied the end of each rope to each of the sow's hind legs. He then tied the remaining ends to one of each of the shoats' hind legs. "Now you fellers won't go very far," he mumbled, stepping back to admire the work of a genius. "I should have thought of that beforehand. Then I could have slept all day." He knew that the cows weren't as apt to stray as far away as the hogs were, and the hogs could not stray very far, trussed up like they were. "Now I'll catch another nap of sleep. I'll check on you later on," he said, patting the sow's side.

Clem went back into the house and lay down on a pile of soft quilts in a corner of a bedroom. After only a few minutes of complete quiet, he fell into a deep, restful sleep for the second time that day.

*   *   *   *

After a long, relaxing sleep, Clem awoke to a chorus of hogs squealing and a dog barking. He ran outside and found Old Bowser running around and barking at the hogs. The baying made the squeals grow in magnitude

When Bart overtook Dump, he said that he had used sugar from their mother's sugar bowl to feed to the horse. He had been doing that for the past week. He wanted to be able to catch the horse without a lot of effort. "I just made up that story about a snake charming him," Bart admitted.

"Ever'body knew that," Dump came back. "You can't tell a tale like that and keep a straight face. You told it in such a way that it was entertaining, though."

*　　*　　*　　*

"Did the snake really charm Ol' Jock, Clem?" Teed asked after Dump and Bart went up on the hill behind the barn to cut the wagon wheels. He watched the progress made in constructing the wagon body. The kid was so little and gullible that he would believe anything the older brothers told him. He gazed toward the hill behind the barn, hoping to see his big brothers returning with a log.

"You know that snakes don't charm animals. They just charm people is all," Clem came back, smiling at Teed.

Judge L. took a homemade corncob pipe from his mouth, spat on the ground like he had seen his Uncle Barney do, then looked at Clem. He thought for a moment, holding the pipe in his right hand, then said, "Brother, you know very well that snakes can't charm people, or animals, and don't you believe that they can."

Judge L. was too young to smoke a pipe, but he had always said that he intended to smoke a fine pipe when he got old enough. He was only practicing holding it in his mouth to be ready when the big day came. He would have looked odd without his ever-present pipe gripped firmly between his teeth.

"Let's get back to work on this wagon while Dump and Bart cut the tree for the wheels," Jake suggested.

"Look here, Jake," Clem snapped, showing his inherited authority, "I give the orders when Dump's gone, and don't you forget it."

"Little Boss!" Teed yelled, jumping up and down and pointing at Clem.

"Dump was right when he said that you should go to the house and suck your bottle!" Clem retorted. "Why don't you do that. And have Mom change your diaper while you're there, Teed."

"We're gonna make a wagon. We're gonna make a wagon. We're gonna make a wagon, with Little Boss giving orders," Teed chanted, jumping up and down. "You can't run me off, Clem. You can say anything about me that you want to, but it won't make me mad enough to leave. I'm gonna stick to you like a leech on a lizard." He continued to jump up and down and run around the work area, chanting, "We're gonna make a wagon."

"You can stay with us, but stay out of our hair," Clem ordered.

"Clem, how do you think Bart caught Ol' Jock?" Jake queried.

"I don't have the vaguest idee, Jake," Clem said. "Dump will find out. He'll pump it out of Bart. Dump would make a good lawyer."

"Dump will make Bart talk," Teed chimed. "Dump's a lawyer."

"He's not a lawyer, Teed," Jake said. "Clem just said that Dump would make a good lawyer—you little nut. Here they come with the log," he said, pointing toward the wood lot.

"Just in time, too," Clem said, driving the last nail into the wide board, attaching it to the rear axle of the wagon body.

Dump and Bart came down the lane with a black gum log about eighteen inches in diameter and ten feet long.

Old Jock dug his feet into the soft dirt as he strained against his collar. The log followed the plodding horse, cutting a groove into the ground as it was pulled along the path.

Dump could be heard clucking to Old Jock and yelling at him to make him speed up a little.

Bart walked along behind Dump, stepping with an unsteady pace, trying to catch the end of a trailing check line with a bare foot, hoping to jerk the line out of his unsuspecting brother's hand.

Bart finally caught one of the lines under his foot. That caused Dump to lose control of the horse as the check line was pulled out of his hand, causing the horse's head to turn to one side, stopping him in his tracks. Bart ran back up the lane to avoid being hit by a lump of dirt that Dump chucked at him and ducked just in time to avoid the earthen projectile.

After a brief rest, Dump clucked Old Jock into movement again and went on toward the blacksmith shop.

Teed was so excited and caught up in the thought of getting a chance to ride the humongous wagon that he forgot that Jake had called him a nut. "How did Bart catch Ol' Jock so easy," he asked when Dump stopped the tired horse.

Old Jock was breathing hard—like a bee smoker—his sides going in and out. His nostrils flared, and sweat dripped off his soft, moist nose.

"Teed, are you still here asking silly questions?" Dump wanted to know. He unhitched Ol' Jock from the log, took the tow chain from around the end of the log, and told Bart to unharness the horse and turn him into the pasture.

"No, I'm not here. I've gone digging for gold around in the Barn Holler," Teed answered, giggling. "Can't you see me standing right here in front of you, Dump?"

"I see too much of you," Dump grumbled. "And if you don't get out of the way and quit asking so many questions, I'm gonna lock you in the hen-house with that old settin' hen and her chickey-diddles. Now scat on out of here and let us get to work."

Teed sat on a rock and watched. He was at that question-asking age and had not found the person who could answer all his questions. No one should blame him for wanting to know things, even though he asked his questions at the wrong time. How could a child learn if he could not ask questions? No one would volunteer the information that he was continuously seeking.

"How did Bart catch Ol' Jock?" Clem prodded Dump.

"He said that he's been sneaking sugar out of Mom's sugar bowl and feeding it to Ol' Jock," Dump replied while using a cant hook, a tool used to grip and roll logs, to roll the log into position. He stood the cant hook on its pointed end and leaned the handle against the wall of the blacksmith shop. He picked up a crosscut saw and motioned for Clem to take one end of it. "Here, help me saw the wheels, Clem," he said.

With each boy gripping a handle of the saw, they commenced their work, making the teeth cut into the tough wood as they pulled the saw back and forth over the rough, uneven surface of the log. Long slivers of sawdust fell to the ground, landing on a growing pile, resembling a bunch of long white worms as the cutting teeth bit into the wood and the drag teeth pulled the cuttings out of the way. They sawed a two-inch-wide cut out of the tree to make the first wheel for their humongous wagon.

"I'm tired of having to run that devilish, wild horse ever' time I have to catch him. I tamed him with sugar," Bart explained. "Would you fellers have thought of something as simple as that—taming a horse with sugar?"

"Mom'll tame *you* if she finds out that you've been feeding her sugar to a horse," Clem said.

There was much more conversation—arguing and joking—about catching the horse and snake charmings. The boys finished the wagon, then took a moment to admire their handiwork.

"Teed, you've been wanting to help. I've got a good job for you to do," Dump said, grinning sneakily.

"Good!" Teed shouted. "You name it and I'll do it. What do you want this eager beaver to do?" he asked, jumping up and down excitedly. He was finally able to help do something constructive in the wagon-building project.

"You can gather up all the tools and put them where they belong," Dump said, laughing at the disappointment that showed on Teed's crest-fallen face. "Then you can pick up all the scraps of planks and carry them to the house for Mom to use for stove wood."

"I don't want to do that," Teed whined, looking at his big brother, hoping that Dump was only joshing with him and would clean up the scraps of wood himself.

"Well, it's either that or no riding down the mountain on our wagon," Dump replied, looking at his handiwork—the huge, clumsy cart.

"All right, I'll do it, but under protest, mind you," the little fellow snapped, repeating a phrase that he had heard his father use when he talked about doing work in the mines which was supposed to be another man's job. Teed wanted to ride that wagon. It was big enough to accommodate five passengers—all at the same time!

While in the woods cutting the tree for the wagon wheels, Dump and Bart had cooked up a plan to have some fun with Judge L. Their scheme was to have Judge L. act as the brakeman on the wagon. They approached their younger brother with their plan.

"Now, Judge L.," Bart began, unable to hide a big grin of delight, "you can be our brakeman when we ride this humongous wagon down Grandpa's pasture field."

"I don't want to be your brakeman. Let Clem do it, or Jake, or Dump, or you, Bart. Why me? I'm the littlest one in the bunch, except for Teed," he grumbled, his face turning red with anger. He knew that Bart was setting him up for something, but he didn't know what.

Each year Judge L. had his hair cut down to the scalp as soon as school ended for the summer vacation. He said that it was easier to wash his head when he had no hair. He looked comical when he was mad, as he was right then, and with no hair on his shining head, he looked even more comical than usual.

"We'll let the wagon be a freight train. You can be the brakeman on my train," Dump offered.

"*Your* train?" Bart exclaimed. "I thought it was *our* train!"

"It's our train, but I'm the engineer," Dump said.

"Engineer Dump," Teed laughed, jumping up and down. The kid was always jumping up and down. He was so hyper.

"I'm Engineer Cornfield," Dump reported.

"I'll be the conductor," Bart volunteered. "Step right up, folks. Hand me your tickets and board the ol' Coaley Creek Spacial, going to places unknown. Watch your steps as you board 'er. Where are your tickets, folks? Step lively there, little bald-headed boy."

Judge L. frowned at Bart and sat down on the wagon.

"I'll be head-end brakeman," Jake announced.

"I'll be a hobo," Clem laughed, pulling his shirt out of his pants. He rubbed dirt on his arms and face to give him a dirty, hobo appearance.

"I'll be a hobo, too—just like Clem," Teed added, continuing his excited jumping about.

"No, you won't," Dump protested. "You're too little, Teed. You might get hurt. Dad would tan all of our hides with a two-handed brash if you were to ride and get hurt."

"I'm allus too little to do anything," Teed whined, ready to burst out crying.

"You can do the cheering for us," Dump told him, patting him on the head.

"Yeah, go and get Skatney, Gillis, and Friday," Clem said. "You kids can do some cheering as we go to the top of the hill to make our train ride down."

"Ain't you gonna make a trial run on a little hill before you take your ride on a big hill?" Teed queried. "It might fall apart on you and hurt ever'-body real bad. Then I'd have to put it back together and ride it all by myself. You all would all be hurt and crying around and couldn't do any riding down the hill."

"Teed has the duck soup churning in his head," Bart laughed.

"Yeah, you fellers had better watch out," Clem agreed. "If Teed starts to thinking real hard, his head could 'splode all over us."

Teed thought that his idea was a good one, but his brothers laughed at him. "Go ahead and laugh all you want to," he whined. "There'll come a time when you'll 'member that I told you boys that you should make a trial run."

"Go on and get Skatney, Gillis, and Friday to do the cheering," Dump prompted.

"Good idee!" Teed shouted, running to his two sisters and his little brother, quickly forgetting that the others had chided him for his suggestion.

The five brothers groaned and grunted while moving the wagon—some pushing and others pulling—to the of the hill enjoy a brief race to the valley below.

*　*　*　*

"We can do the cheering for the ride off Grandpa's pasture," Teed explained to Skatney as they raced to the site of the wagon ride.

"You know the football cheers that we've been practicing, don't you?" Skatney said. "We can do them."

"But it ain't a football game," Gillis panted, almost out of breath from trying to keep up.

"We'll change them from football cheers to freight train cheers. We can do them the same way," Skatney explained, and the rest agreed.

"Wait for me!" Friday begged, struggling along, far behind the bigger siblings, but getting no sympathy from the speeding youngsters.

The tired children arrived at the foot of the steep hill just as the riders reached the top.

"We're gonna cheer!" Skatney yelled, still out of breath.

"Okay! Yell real loud!" came Dump's reply.

"Are you ready?" Skatney asked, turning to the little ones. "You know how we've practiced these cheers before." She started chanting.

"Jump on a freight train!

"Ride on a freight train!

"Run down the hill on a freight train!

"Yea! Yea! Yea!"

Teed, Gillis, and Friday joined in on the second round of cheers.

Engineer Dump gave his crew their instructions. "If we get to going too fast, Judge L., put on the brakes and stop us," he said.

"How can I put on the brakes?" Judge L. asked, looking at Dump for an explanation of his proposed duties. "We don't have a brake pedal or brake lever on this clumsy vehicle."

"I'll tell you how fer to do it if we need brakes," Bart offered. "Just don't worry that pretty bald head."

"I'm not worrying my bald head—I'm just worrying about stopping this wagon if you holler for brakes. You all'll have to do some helping me."

"We'll help you," Bart promised, smiling. He almost laughed.

Bart's promise to help seemed to relax Judge L. just a little. He raised his feet off the ground as the wagon started to move.

"I'm in full throttle," Dump informed his unprepared crew.

Away they went. And the farther they went, the faster they went. They surely had a good wagon!

Skatney, Teed, Gillis, and Friday continued to chant encouragement.

The wagoners bumped along over the rough slope, running at break-neck speed, splattering cow patties in their way. The manure caught on the moving wheels and was thrown onto the backs of the riders, making big splotches on their faded chambray shirts and plastering their hair to their heads.

Dense clumps of blackberry briars flew by as Dump tried to maneuver the clumsy cart through the slalom-like course. He used his feet to steer the wagon while holding the tow rope tightly in his hands. The crowd behind him gave him no help. His legs were almost at an upright position, taking away most of his steering abilities. With Jake hanging on for dear life, Dump's arm movements were limited to almost none at all.

Engineer Dump saw the split-rail fence that separated the pasture from Grandpa's bull-lot come racing to meet the humongous wagon. "Brakes!" he shouted. "Apply the brakes, Judge L.!"

"How can I?" Judge L. asked, trying to look ahead. His view was blocked by a bunch of brothers.

"Grab the rear wheels. That'll stop us," Bart shouted.

Judge L. did as he was instructed. He grabbed the moving wheels. As he gripped the rolling disks, his hands were pulled beneath them, forming scotches. He began to scream like a wildcat.

Realizing that Judge L. could not stop their forward motion, Dump yelled, "Jump!" and rolled off the speeding wagon.

Judge L. was the only one unable to jump. He was left alone, held by the wagon's wheels. Finally, with the weight of the other boys gone, Judge L. was able to pull his hands free and roll off, just as the wagon rammed the fence, breaking the rails into kindling-wood.

The awkward cart continued to roll through the bull-lot and came to rest, nose first, in the stream that ran through the field.

Judge L. stood up and grimaced with pain. He held his hands out where he could see the damage caused by the sliding wheels. He started to slip his hands into his pockets, seeking relief, but changed his mind when the pain became too severe. He walked toward his laughing brothers, holding his hands out as if they were to be inspected by someone.

"You're crazy, Bart," Judge L. whined as he came up to where everyone had gathered, looking at the damage done to the fence. His voice shook with pain and anger.

Bart lay on the ground, kicking and howling with laughter, watching Judge L. through a sea of tears.

Judge L. humped and gimped around in pain. "You're as crazy as can be," he repeated. "Why did you tell me to grab the wheels to stop that big wagon? You knew what would happen to me. You're crazy for telling me to do that."

"You're crazy for doing it," Bart laughed.

"We made a good wagon," Dump mumbled. He spoke to no one in particular.

"I'm hurt, and all you can talk about is that you made a good wagon," Judge L. wailed, still humping and gimping around in pain.

"It wouldn't help your hands any if I said that it was a bad wagon," Dump said. "I never thought about that fence," he continued. "I guess we have a big job of splitting fence rails to replace the one's that we destroyed." He wiped his hair and shirt with a bunch of leaves he had picked from a poplar bush that grew in the fence row.

"I guess we ought to tell Dad about tearing up the fence," Clem mentioned, pulling a bunch of leaves from a sassafras bush, giving his hair a healthy rubbing.

"Dad don't need to know about this, boys," Dump stated, nervous with the thought of his father finding out about the damage to the fence. "Who's gonna tell on his own self? We're all in this together, you know."

Everyone looked at Dump and shrugged his shoulders, indicating that there would be no volunteers to step forward. No one was going to tell.

No one?

Teed would carry the message. "I ain't in any trouble," Teed said. "You wouldn't let me help build the wagon or let me ride it, either, so I'll tell Dad." He turned and raced toward the house.

"Come back here!" Dump said, running after Teed, trying to catch the little boy. Dump was just a little too slow.

Teed was really hotfooting it in his effort to tattle to his father. He had finally found something that he could do well. Tattling wasn't the most exciting thing that he could do, concerning that humongous wagon, but tattling was better than nothing.

Celebrating Corn Laid By

Teed disliked hoeing corn worse than any job on the farm. No. He had rather hoe corn than hoe potatoes. Well, maybe it was a toss-up between the two. Frankly, Teed did not like farm work, period. He enjoyed playing much better than working, any old time.

Teed's father was a fairly adept hillside farmer. He never went by the signs when he planted his crops, as did so many old-timers in his neighborhood, although he wanted to. Marn's work in the coal mines cramped his schedule during the springtime. He had to plant when he got his chance—when the ground was warm and dry. "When I get ready to plant, the signs and the moon will have to be ready if they want to have anything to do with making my taters grow," Marn often said. He told other people, those who went by the signs, religiously, that he didn't plant on the moon—he planted in the ground.

The crops were planted early, since Marn worked in the mines. After the early planting was done, Marn went back to Jenkins, Kentucky, to work, staying from Sunday evening to Friday, boarding with a cousin, coming home on weekends to be with the family for a short time and to check up on the crops and livestock.

The corn, potatoes, oats, and the two big vegetable gardens, truck patches, as Marn called them, grew with a vigor and flourished in the warm spring weather.

School was out for the smaller kids. The older boys and girls had finished the sixth grade. When they passed to the seventh grade, their formal education ended, since the nearest high school was nearly ten miles away and there was no school bus to transport the children to and from the high school at Big Onion Gap.

Marn and Vann figured that the boys could work in the coal mines, as Marn had always done, and the girls could marry men who were already employed as miners, thus making a good living by digging the fossil fuel.

Coal mining and small-crop farming had always been the livelihood for the Cornfields.

The boys were really too young to work inside the mines, so they had to take care of the farm while Marn was away from home.

"Jake," Judge L. said, spreading big globs of flour-gravy over two torn up biscuits one midsummer evening, "do you want to help me dig that treasure up tomorrow morning?"

"I sure do," Jake answered around a mouthful of half-chewed food. "Since we don't have to go to school, we should have plenty time to dig up that big treasure and become rich folks."

The family sat at the supper table that Sunday evening. Everyone slurped and gnyammed as he filled his stomach to the bursting point with good, wholesome food.

"What treasure?" Bart asked, looking at Judge L. with interest.

"You know the one I'm talking about, Bart. It's the last one we found— over in the holler below Isome Gap," Judge L. said, giving Bart the location of the treasure site. "The place where them four trees are planted in a perfect square. Somebody sure knew what he was doing when he planted them trees like that. You can tell that they was planted in a square that way for a purpose. We're gonna find out the why for they planted them there like that as soon as we dig it up. Inside that square are three rocks that form a prefect triangle."

"I've seen them trees before, and they ain't in a perfect square. All the sides of a square are the same length." Bart laughed.

"Well, it looks like a perfect square to me," Judge L. came back, smiling at Bart. "Anyway, there has to be some Indian treasure buried there. Or maybe a bank robber buried a heist there and never come back to claim it. There's just got to be a treasure somewhere amongst the trees and rocks. Nature couldn't have planted the trees and placed the rocks there the way they are."

"Who in this area had anything that was worth enough to hide for protection?" Beaut asked, a smile of wonder spreading over her pretty face.

"It could have been the Rebels that took gold from the Union during the Civil War and hid the gold so that they could have it to get a good start in life after the war," Judge L. surmised.

"I'm sure they had a big Civil War battle over there around Isome Gap!" Bart said, a touch of sarcasm etching his voice.

"Well, it could have happened that way," Judge L. replied impetuously.

"We'll start on that digging first thing Monday morning," Jake said. "By the way," he continued, "tomorrow's Monday. We're gonna be rich sooner than you expected, Judge L. We'll go by and get Esker Seedy, then on over to Uncle Sturble's house and get Cousin Jubal, too. I think Jubal was with Esker when he found the treasure site."

"I know what I'm gonna buy with my big share of the treasure," Judge L. said. "I'm gonna buy me a new bicycle, a full-sized one that I saw in the catalog. It's on page 1036—left-hand corner of the right-hand page."

"You ain't been looking in the catalog much, have you?" Bart chuckled.

"Not much," Judge L. replied. "I just remember that there was a purty bicycle on that page. Numbers come easy for me to remember. That's why I'm real good in mathematics."

"I'm gonna get me a bicycle just like the one that you're gonna get, Judge L.," Teed said, getting into the conversation with the big boys. "I'm good in mathematics, too."

"You can't get a bicycle, Teed," Judge L. told him. "You need lots of money to buy a bicycle like mine, and I know that you don't have any money at all."

"I've got just as much money as you have—maybe more!" Teed stormed. "You ain't rolling in dough yourself."

"No, you don't have as much money as I have, Teed," Judge L. argued. "You don't have a treasure to dig up like I have."

"I'll help you dig up your treasure and share it with you," Teed suggested, smiling around the table at each brother and sister.

"I ain't sharing my hard-earned treasure with a snot-nosed kid like you," Judge L. came back. "If I have to work hard to dig it up, you ain't gonna get any of it, and you can bank on that."

"If I help dig it up, I'll be doing just as much work as you," Teed reasoned. "Dad and Mom's allus told us children to share with one another, and I think that now is the time for us to do what they have told us to do. So, both of us can have a bicycle if we share the treasure. Don't be so stingy. The treasure ain't any more yours than it's mine. It belongs to somebody else if they hid it over there at Isome Gap."

"Why do you want a bicycle, Teed?" Beaut asked, attempting to break up the little, harmless argument between Teed and Judge L.

"I just need a bicycle like the one that Judge L. is gonna get is all," Teed answered. "The way I look at is that I don't think that he should buy a bicycle and try to keep me from doing the same thing. We're both gonna have lots of money with that big treasure. It ain't his money that I'll be spending, even though he acts like it's coming out of his pocket. I don't see where he gets his gripe."

"He wants a bicycle so he can ride it to go see Zel Seedy," Judge L. teased, and everyone laughed.

"No, I don't want to see Zel Seedy!" Teed blurted out, his face turning red with anger. "I hate that old ugly girl."

"Teed wants to see Zel Seedy and court her and kiss her on the lips," Judge L. said, laughing along with the rest of the family.

"She's too ugly. She dips snuff, and I don't want a snuff dipper for a sweetheart!" Teed shouted in anger, ready to cry. "She's like her mother," he continued. "They both dip snuff, and Esker and Tester chew 'backer all the time. I wouldn't kiss Zel Seedy, and you can smoke that in your empty pipe, Judge L. I'd just as soon kiss a cow on the lips!"

"Who's ever seen a cow's lips?" Judge L. asked, pecking the table with his empty corncob pipe. "Teed could kiss cow-lips Zel Seedy."

Teed was getting mad. He thought that it was about time for his father to intervene in the conversation.

Marn was smiling and enjoying himself while listening to the older boys kid Teed. He was amused with the thought of Teed kissing Zel Seedy.

Zel Seedy was an ugly girl. She was as homely as they made little girls. The ugly bug probably bit her often during her first years. She could not help that, of course, but her handicap did not get any sympathy from Teed. He could not understand why his brothers picked such an unsightly girl to tease him about. He didn't claim her, but they teased him as if he did. He couldn't stand the girl.

Teed remembered him and Gillis washing their hands for supper one evening. He was mad because his brothers were teasing him about that ugly little girl, and instead of asking for the soap, he said, "Give me the Zel, Gillis." It made no difference how hard he tried, and he had tried his best, he could never live down that one little slip of the tongue.

"Boys," Marn intervened, speaking to the older lads, "you leave Teed alone, and I'll tell you where you can dig a big pile of treasure. It's real close by, too. It ain't as far away as Isome Gap. I've had my eye on this treasure for the last few weeks. I ain't had time to dig for it. With my job in the mines, I've just not had time to dig for big fortunes. I think I'll dig for treasure tomorrow, then go back to work in the mines Tuesday."

"Why are you going to dig treasure tomorrow and then go did coal?" Judge L. asked. "You should have enough money from your treasure to buy a truck and a car and a level Tennessee farm. Actually, you won't need a big farm to work on—with all that treasure you've got. Maybe you'll want a farm just to graze your riding horses on. Then you could retire Ol' Jock. I had rather have a bicycle than a horse to ride, myself. All that I would have to do is clean it by wiping it off ever' time I ride it around the yard and up and down the holler."

"I could wipe mine clean, too, just like Judge L.," Teed daydreamed.

"Teed, you don't have a bicycle to wipe," Judge L. told him.

"You don't, either," Teed returned. Judge L. was beginning to get on his nerves. Why couldn't he have the same kind of bicycle that Judge L. wanted? Surely there would be enough money for everyone when the treasure was dug up and cashed in.

Teed had already decided what he would do to make his bicycle prettier than Judge L.'s. He would, he decided, put streamers on the handlebars, reflectors on the wheel spokes and fenders, and, just maybe, he would get two black mud-flaps with a big bunch of reflectors on them, too. He would have a better bicycle than Judge L. could ever think of having.

Jake had not said anything else, nor had the rest of the brothers and sisters.

Teed couldn't understand why they weren't excited about their father's treasure. He asked Dump what he intended to buy with his share.

Dump smiled and said, "I've not decided yet. I just can't make up my mind. There are so many things I want."

"I've made up my mind," Teed said excitedly. "I might even share my part with Gillis."

That got a smile from Gillis, who, up until then, had not said anything or shown any excitement. Maybe he did not realize what a treasure was, since he was so young. He probably did not realize that the Cornfield family was going to be rich people as soon as they dug up that treasure and cashed it at the bank at Big Onion Gap.

"You young 'uns get your chores done and get ready for bed early," Marn ordered. "You'll need a lot of sleep and rest for tomorrow. We've got to get out early in the morning and get to digging for treasure. Ever'body'll have to be ready to start early. We may have to dig all day, right up till dark, to get to the treasure." With those last words about treasure, Marn rose from the table and left the room.

*   *   *   *

Teed lay awake for hours that night, thinking of the treasure and how he was going to spend his share. "Gillis, are you asleep?" he asked, punching his little brother in the ribs.

"Sleep...yeah," he said, smacking his lips to clear the bad sleep taste from his dry mouth. He turned over and snuggled down under the single sheet on the bed.

"What are you going to buy with your part of the treasure?" Teed asked.

"Yeah, treasure...buy...dig...bicycle...." Gillis mumbled indistinctly, then began to snore as he again fell into a deep, peaceful sleep.

How could Gillis sleep at a time like that, Teed wondered? He also wondered if Judge L. was asleep or awake, thinking.

Finally, Teed drifted off to sleep…riding that beautiful bicycle, on page 1036 in the Sears and Roebuck catalogue, down the path to the pig-lot. He rode along as smooth as a cloud on the wind—just floating along. The bicycle was a fine piece of machinery.

The peddling slowed, becoming sluggish. When Teed looked down at the reflector-covered wheels, he saw that they were covered with mud from the pig wallows. The mud became so thick and gooey that he lost the bicycle in a deep puddle of the guck. He lay in the mud, next to the bicycle. Each time he reached for the handlebars, the bicycle slid deeper into the gooey mess. Teed was helplessly stuck in the mud, still reaching for the bicycle that was slowly slipping away from him.

Judge L. appeared on the opposite side of the mud-hole and began to laugh.

The pigs lined up in an even row and laughed along with Judge L.

"Help me, Judge L.!" Teed yelled.

The pigs echoed Teed's plea for help by saying, "Help me Judge L."

"Sorry, I can't reach you," Judge L. told him.

"Sorry, I can't reach you," the pigs said, grunting, snorting, and laughing in pig language, blowing pig snot and slobber over the sinking bicycle.

"Help me Judge L.," Teed repeated as the bicycle sank deeper into the mud.

"Might get mud and guck on me," Judge L. told him, laughing harder.

"Might get mud and guck on me," the pigs said, echoing Judge L.'s reply, continuing to pig laugh.

Teed's last attempt to secure a hold on the handlebars ended as he fell into the mud, which turned out to be the floor of his bedroom. He had been dreaming and had fallen out of his bed. What a nightmare!

Marn entered the room just as Teed hit the floor with a thud. "Rise and shine, treasure diggers," he ordered. "I see that Teed's already up. The rest of you should show some excitement? Shake a leg now!" He went back into the kitchen.

Teed groped about in the early morning darkness in search of his clothes. He had slept very little that night. He tried to rub the sleep from his eyes as he entered the kitchen. The bright light from the kerosene lamp hit his irritated eyes with a blinding glare, causing him to close them to shut out the light while he stumbled about in search of the wash pan.

Breakfast was like a dream. Teed was sleepy, but the rest of the family was having a good time joking, laughing, and eating a good meal.

"We won't plow the corn out this time," Marn informed the family. "We'll cut the weeds and dig a little dirt to each hill."

"I thought we was gonna did for treasure today, Dad," Judge L. whined, disappointment showing in his voice.

"We are," Marn said. "The treasure is a field of corn. You can't dig treasure from the ground without first putting something into it to dig out. Our treasure will be in the corn we grow for bread and feed for the livestock. We'll get something from each of the animals."

"Yeah, I stepped in what you get out of cows and chickens just yesterday when I done my chores," Judge L. whined.

"Boys, remember this. You can only get out of life what you put into it," Marn said soberly. "You can get real hungry waiting for riches to come by and lay right down in front of you. So let's get in that field and dig a real treasure. Let this be a lesson to you squirts. You can't get a bicycle without hard work."

Marn and the older children left the room, while Judge L. and Teed sat there in a daze. They could hardly get in gear so early in the morning. They finally left the table to join the rest, on their way to the cornfield.

* * * *

That cornfield looked huge and unending. The rows seemed to stretch away from Teed as he worked toward the opposite end of the field. He had lost sleep for nothing. He expected to get a treasure. He got a field of corn, weeds, and packsaddles instead. He hated packsaddles, weeds, corn, and working in corn. Right then he hated everything that was related to corn and work.

Teed chopped weeds, dug dirt, and watched for packsaddles and other stinging worms. He had already been stung several times. He grunted, scratched, gimped, and almost cried. He was disgusted with everything, especially packsaddles with their many painful stingers. He spent more time lookin for the green worm with reddish-brown spots on its back, resembling a horse's saddle, than he spent hoeing corn.

From where Teed was working, the field seemed to stretch to the very edge of eternity, and that is a long way for anything to stretch. After what seemed like a long week to Teed, the top of the field was there in front of the diligent workers. At last Teed could finally become acquainted with that last row, so far from the bottom of the field.

Bart was still happy and full of fun. "See that big log up there in the edge of the woods?" he said, pointing toward the end of the field, where a huge chestnut tree had fallen many years earlier. "Let's climb on that log and yell real loud to celebrate laying by this field of corn."

"That's a good idee," Dump said, racing toward the log. He was joined by the rest of the brothers and sisters. They perched on the fallen tree like a flock of turkeys on a roost.

In his mad dash for a position on the log, unbeknownst to the other jubilant boys and girls, Bart had scooped up a handful of soft, fine dirt, and as Judge L. yelled with his mouth wide-open, the mischievous Bart pitched the entire handful of dirt into the open cavern.

The scream changed to gagging and spitting as Judge L. attempted to clear his mouth and throat of the dirt. "I'll get you for that," he said as he spat the last of the lumps of dirt from his mouth. He gagged and spat once more, then turned to Jake with his hoe raised.

Jake was too fast, though. He was soon far ahead of mad Judge L.

Bart laughed so hard that he lost his breath and began to dry-heave and gasp for fresh air.

Dump, Beaut, Clem, Skatney, Teed, and Gillis laughed along with Bart.

Bart threw the dirt, but Jake had to run to evade an attack from Judge L., who thought that Jake had done it.

Judge L. continued to scream at Jake as the two raced toward the house.

A Busted Head

Everyone had heard the news about Talmage Seedy, an elderly man who lived on Coaley Creek.

Teed Cornfield remembered the incident in which the man was seriously injured. The boy saw Talmage as an old person. Teed was just a kid when the accident happened, and to a child all grown-ups look old.

Talmage Seedy, like most of the men on Coaley Creek, liked to partake of a little nip of strong drink occasionally, but in his case—often—often enough to get a little tipsy. Sometimes he got tipsy enough to topple.

One Sunday afternoon, after having partaken of some strong liquid, Talmage Seedy was at Baggley Cornfield's house, probably to get more to drink. Everyone knew where to get a snort when he needed one. Talmage was feeling very "good" that Sunday afternoon. While loosely mounted on his trusty steed, Old Trevor, he gave the horse a sudden goading with his heels, causing the horse to run up the hill at his fastest pace. Talmage's feet were out of the stirrups at the time, and he was hanging on to the bridle reins for dear life.

Old Trevor was a high-spirited horse. That afternoon he was at his highest spirits, but not in the same high spirits as his master. Old Trevor was in his running spirits, while Talmage was in his drinking spirits. Old Trevor was really picking his feet up and putting them back down as he ran up the hill.

Talmage lost control of the bridle reins and rolled backward off Old Trevor's back and landed smack-dab on a big flat rock, where water, during rainy weather, had washed the dirt away, leaving a bare slab of sandstone outcropping in the middle of the narrow road.

The horse tried to jump the rock to avoid stepping on it. Talmage had lost control of his horse when the wild leap occurred without his being ready for any sudden change of pace.

One must give Talmage a little credit for his good horsemanship, though, for he was a good rider when sober, but he was completely off balance that day due to the lack of body control—and horse control.

Talmage smacked the rock a resounding blow with the back of his head. It made such a loud noise that Teed heard it a long distance from the site of the mishap.

Teed and the rest of his family were in the lower garden, right across from their Uncle Baggley's barn. The children were gathering vegetables to be canned and dried for winter storage.

When Talmage Seedy struck Old Trevor a sudden blow with his heels, it made the horse give a loud snort. That was what got everyone's attention. The boys were laughing uproariously when they heard the smack of Talmage's head on the rock. The sound alone told the boys that Talmage was probably seriously hurt. They ran to help Uncle Baggley in any way they could.

Uncle Baggley began to yell for his sons, Shade and Sonny, to come and help him with Talmage. He figured that Talmage had burst his head. "It ain't cracked plum' open, but it must be busted. Talmage hit smack-dab on that big rock!" he yelled.

Shade and Sonny couldn't have heard Baggley's plea for help, for they were in the house.

Teed and his brothers arrived at the barn in a matter of minutes— Dump in the lead, as usual, followed closely by the rest.

Talmage Seedy lay on the rock where he had fallen—deathly still. His eyes were closed. Tears had puddled up in the corners of his eyes next to his nose. The presence of death hovered over the barnyard.

Uncle Baggley continued to jump and hop around excitedly, gripping his knees from time to time. That was his habit when he was overly excited.

"What must we do?" Uncle Baggley asked as Dump and the rest stood around with their hands in their pockets, wondering what to do. "Should we move him, Dump? Should we get him inside the house with a soft piller under his head?"

"I really don't think he should be moved real quick," Dump replied.

"I've read that when a person falls that way, he can get a concussion of the skull or brain. Let me go get help for him. I'll get his family and then ride to Big Onion Gap and get Doc Buckles to come and see about Talmage. Don't move him while I'm gone. Just make him as comfortable as you can till help arrives."

"Go get Marn," Uncle Baggley pleaded. "Tell him that we need him bad. He's allus got a calm head on his shoulders."

"Dad's at work. Clem, you and the other boys get Cousin Shade and Cousin Sonny out of the house and over here to help Uncle Baggley," Dump ordered the younger brothers. "Then go on home and tell Mom. She'll probably come down here and help out. She's real good with sick folks." He mounted Old Trevor and headed up the path, aware of the big rock in the way, on his way to get help.

Clem, Bart, Jake, Teed, Gillis, and Judge L. stopped at Uncle Baggley's house to tell Cousin Shade and Cousin Sonny to go help with Talmage Seedy. After the boys had delivered the message, they went on to their house and reported the news of Talmage Seedy's fall.

Vann Cornfield received the news and stood silently for a few minutes, looking at the floor. With a grave expression she replied, "It's a caution that he has gone this long without falling off that horse and getting hisself killed dead. Maybe this will be the lesson that will stop him from drinking so much. I don't see how his wife, Sadie, can accept the way he drinks all the time. She has to be a patient wife—almost a saint—to put up with that stupid drinking. I'll have to send Beaut down there to help out for a few days. That poor woman can't take care of Talmage and all them young 'uns by herself."

*   *   *   *

Talmage Seedy lay in a coma for many days, and, at times, in a semiconscious state. His condition was very grave. The doctor made a house call and checked out the man's injury—a concussion was the diagnosis. He told the family to keep Talmage in bed until he came out of the coma. The doctor made no bones about the severity of the concussion. He did not paint any rosy pictures of the eventual outcome of the man's plight. He told the Seedys to follow his instructions to the tee; if they did not adhere to them, there would be no need to come for his help again in the future. Talmage Seedy would be a statistic on Coaley Creek.

*   *   *   *

Esker Seedy, Talmage's next-to-the-oldest son, met Teed and Gillis at the door one day, about a week after the near-fatal accident. "Did you ever see a busted noggin, Teed?" he asked after he greeted the brothers and invited them to come into the house, where his father lay in bed in the big front room.

"Yeah, I have," Teed told him. "I saw your dad at Uncle Baggley's house when he fell off Ol' Trevor and busted his head on that rock in the road. We had to go home before help came to take Talmage to the doctor or hospital, or wherever you took him. Did you take him to the hospital?"

"No, we didn't take him to the hospital," Esker answered. "If we had took him to the hospital, he wouldn't be in as good a shape as he's in right now. He'd probably have died from jostling around in your uncle's wagon bed. Your Uncle Baggley brought Dad home in a two-horse wagon on a feather bed. We didn't take him to the hospital. We was afraid that the rough ride in the wagon over the rocky road would hurt his head much worse than it was. Come on in and look at him. You can't look inside his head and see anything. It ain't like a busted punkin or squash. It didn't break open and spill his brain out. Teed, did you know that your skin holds all your bones in place and keeps them from falling out?"

"Everybody knows that," Gillis replied. "Don't they, Teed?"

"S'pose so," Teed said, following Esker into the silent house, where Talmage Seedy lay in bed, his head resting on a big feather pillow.

There was no movement at all from the man. Only the slow rise and fall of his chest indicated that there was a little life in the still form. He looked dead as he lay there with his eyes closed.

"Dump told me and Teed that your dad has a concoction," Gillis said. He peered at Talmage Seedy, searching for a crack in the still man's head. The little fellow had never seen a concoction before.

"What's a concoction?" Esker asked, directing his question to Gillis.

"He ain't got a concoction, Gillis. He's got a concussion," Teed corrected his brother. "He don't know anything. He's too little to know much," Teed apologized, turning to face Esker.

"He's almost dead, Esker," Gillis said, staring intently at Talmage.

"Don't say that, Gillis!" Teed retorted. "The family's worried enough without being reminded that Talmage looks like he's dead. Even though he does, try to have a little more control over your tongue."

"That's all right, Teed," Esker whispered. "When he grows up a little more, he can think without saying ever'thing that comes into his head. Children allus say what they're thinking. Don't worry about it. Folks are allus saying things about his condition—that they really shouldn't say—but we're getting used to it now. We get hurt all the time by what people say, but that's all right. We're getting to where we don't pay much attention to it. People are just unthoughted is all."

"He sure looks dead to me," Gillis declared, turning to leave the room.

Esker and Teed followed Gillis outside, tiptoeing to keep from disturbing the sleeping man. They had talked in whispers while in the room—all except Gillis. Gillis had talked in his normal tone—loud!

Teed and Gillis stayed and played with Esker for a while, staying far enough away from the house to keep from disturbing the sick man. After several hours of intense play, the brothers left Esker standing in his yard with their promise to come again for a day of play and recreation. With that solemn promise they hurried toward home. It was getting late, and they had chores to do.

* * * *

The thought of Talmage Seedy and his concussion just would not leave Teed's mind. He thought about it all the time, especially at night.

"What are your plans for today, Judge L.?" Teed asked while the family ate breakfast early one morning about a week after Talmage Seedy fell from his horse's back and cracked his head.

"I thought that I might get with Esker Seedy and Cousin Jubal and go dig for that treasure over at Isome Gap," Judge L. replied, continuing to eat, talking while chewing his food.

"Good, I'll go with you and help," Teed offered. "I still want that bicycle in the catalog that you picked out on page 1036. I remembered the page number. I'm good at arithmetic since I can remember numbers. I bet you thought that I had forgot about that bicycle, didn't you fellers." He grinned at everyone at the table—one at a time, looking at each person as his gaze went all around the table.

"No, we never forgot about that bicycle. You won't let us forget about it when you talk about it all the time, day in and day out" Judge L. said. "You'll have to stay here. It's a long way over there, and we don't want a little kid tagging along in the way."

"Who's calling who a kid?" Teed asked. "You ain't a grown-up, yourself, and I'm the same age and size as Esker, and I'm almost as big as Cousin Jubal—come all the way up to his shoulder. How come they can go and I can't?"

"They're the ones that found the treasure site, so I have to let them go, but I don't have to let you go," Judge L. reminded Teed.

"Dad, make Judge L. let me go dig treasure with him and Esker Seedy and Cousin Jubal," Teed whined, turning to his father for help.

"Judge L. won't be going to dig for treasure at Isome Gap today," his father replied, rubbing Teed's head. He patted it a few times, then snuffed his head. "You boys will be doing something that'll keep you busy all day."

"I hope we ain't gonna dig for your kind of treasure again, Dad," Judge L. blurted out. "I 'member very distinctly the treasure that you had us hunting for."

"We won't be digging treasure," his father informed him. "Not today, we won't."

"Good!" Judge L. exclaimed. "We can get whatever job you have for us done today and then dig for the treasure tomorrow."

Judge L. just could not understand why Marn kept everyone busy working on the farm all the time instead of letting the boys dig for treasure and get rich. He could not understand why anyone would put working on a rocky hillside farm before digging for treasure.

Marn did not put much stock in a surefire way to get rich. He did not think much of a get-rich-quick scheme. He had rather work for a dollar at a time instead of a big pile of money all at once, especially a hidden treasure on Coaley Creek.

Judge L. figured that he and the rest of the boys could dig for treasure while Marn worked for that dollar at a time if he wanted to.

"Go harness Ol' Jock and Ol' Jack and get the rock-hauling sled out of the shed, Dump," Marn told his eldest son. "I want you boys to move them big rock piles down there in the lower garden today. Haul 'em to the fer-end of the garden next to the hog-lot and pile them along the rail fence. By doing that, we can reinforce the fence and keep the hogs from rooting their way under it."

"All right, Dad," Dump said, obediently rising to start the day's work.

"The rest of you boys do your chores so you can get started moving rocks," Marn ordered. "You know that the sooner you get started, the sooner you'll finish."

"That's good, sound logic," Clem laughed as he followed Dump from the room. "If we don't get started, we won't get done. Come on ever'body. Let's get started so we can get done."

The two boys could be heard laughing at Clem's little quip as they went to the barn.

The work was begun with vigor, but the boys' patience grew thin when they had to wait for only a few minutes while the horses and driver went the few yards to the off-loading spot at the end of the garden. Without the thought of danger they began to throw the smaller rocks to the snake-rail fence.

Gillis hefted a rock that was too big for his size, and when he threw it, Teed was standing right in the line of fire.

The rock struck Teed squarely in the back of the head and knocked him off balance. He staggered around like an addled chicken, a little woozy— not really hurt. He staggered a few extra steps to put on a show for the rest of the group. When he rubbed the knot that had popped up on his head, he felt something wet, and when he inspected his hand, he saw a trace of blood on his index finger.

Talmage Seedy was the first thought that came into Teed's mind. He could see Talmage lying in bed with his eyes closed—as he had seen him that day when he visited Esker. "Oh no! He busted my head!" he cried in panic. Holding his head with both hands, he started to run toward the house, to his mother.

Bart grabbed Teed as the little fellow tried to run past. "Hold on, Teed. You ain't hurt bad," he said, laughing uproariously. "Let me check your noggin. You just scuffed up the rust and dander a little bit is all that's wrong with you." He laughed louder when he found that Teed had only a small scratch. "A little blood's oozing out, but it ain't busted like Talmage Seedy's head. I think you'll live just a little while longer—maybe long enough to get these rocks moved—and if you're lucky enough, you just might grow up to be a big man. Don't fret so much. You're just fine."

"That surely was a close call!" Teed whined, rubbing his hand over the lump. A knot big enough for a goat to nibble had popped up on the back of his head.

That rock-throwing incident wasn't such an amusing thing to Teed, since he had been the recipient of the blow from that big rock that Gillis had hefted in his direction.

That bunch of cutups Teed called brothers certainly thought it was funny. They laughed hilariously, with Bart laughing the hardest of all.

Teed rubbed the knot on his head and started throwing rocks to the hog-lot fence, keeping an eye on Gillis' every move.

One-punch Gillis

Gillis wanted to be a boxer. His lifelong desire was to be a scientific boxer—not a puncher, mind you. He realized that a person could get hurt by hard punches. He knew that he would have to use his head while boxing aggressive opponents—to keep from being punched by them. He figured that he would have to slip in a hard punch once in a while, to let his opponent know that he could punch as well as box. To keep the other fellow off guard, he would have to learn to throw a bunch of hard punches.

Teed taught Gillis just about everything that the kid would ever have to know about boxing—everything that Teed knew about boxing, anyway. He had the kid doing road work by running all the way to Coaley Creek Elementary schoolhouse and back—two miles each way. Teed often told Gillis that something like a lion, panther, wolf, or a "haint" would come out of the laurel thickets and get him, then start running, with Gillis stepping in each track that Teed stepped out of. Teed was fast, but Gillis could keep up with him, step for step.

It is a known fact that all boxers want to be champions, but not all of them want to work hard enough to win a championship. The fact often shows in their performances.

Teed made Gillis work. He told his little brother that if he never became champion, it would not be from the lack of training, so Gillis was given a regimen of rigorous exercises.

Gillis got his interest in—and a start toward—a boxing career during the boxing era of the '40s. He wanted to make something of himself. He lived in the Appalachian Mountains, in the extreme southwestern tip of Virginia.

Appalachia has the richest people in the entire world—barring none, not so much in monetary values as in heritage. People aren't hungry in Appalachia, those on Coaley Creek especially.

Teed was never hungry in his entire life. The only time he ever missed a meal was because he wasn't at home at mealtime. Maybe he did not have the gourmet foods like those the great chefs prepare all over the world, but there was plenty of what he had, and that was something to be grateful for. Teed was just that—very grateful.

Teed had sufficient clothes and shoes to wear. He had a pair of shoes to wear during the summer, if he wanted to, but he liked to go barefooted all summer.

There were several modes of travel in the mountains of Southwest Virginia, from a saddle horse to a covered wagon to a Cadillac car.

Wate Long, a ragtag boy on Coaley Creek, had a Cadillac car. Wate worked in the coal mines, where he made enough money to buy a car, so he chose a Cadillac. It was an old one, but still a Cadillac.

Teed, Gillis, and Satch Hood looked the old car over when Wate Long first traded for it. He traded in a milk cow and a pistol on the car and paid the balance over a four-year period. He never missed a payment during that time. One of the most memorable features about that ancient machine was that a *C* and an *A* were missing from the name on the front of the car. The boys called it a "Dillac" car. They told everyone that they had seen a "Dillac" car. No one believed them, so they had to prove it. They took people to see for themselves, but those who would not take the time to go see the car had to go on disbelieving.

If anyone wanted to be difficult and argue about the car's name, Gillis was ready to settle the matter in the ring. He would agree to fight in an imaginary ring of any size or shape. He didn't care. The kid stayed ready for action.

Teed credited himself for his brother's aggressiveness in a fight. He told Gillis that a fighter should never be awed or cowed by the size, sex, or reputation of his adversaries.

Gillis often challenged far above his potential. He had not found it necessary to meet anyone in combat, though. Just saying that he hankered to be a boxer was usually enough to settle any differences or disagreements that might arise. Those challenges which weren't settled in such a manner ended with Teed talking the bigger boys out of going ahead and giving Gillis a good thrashing.

Teed and Gillis made their own boxing gloves. They used their father's big socks that were too worn to darn, and they didn't give a darn. They used them anyway—by stuffing them with tatters of cloth left over when their mother made clothes for the children.

The boys crammed the pieces of cloth into the old socks, forming cumbersome but safe boxing gloves. They cut holes for their thumbs, making it possible to hold the gloves on their hands. They didn't have tape or strings to hold the gloves in place while sparring in their makeshift ring out behind the smokehouse.

Teed taught his brother how to shadow box, and while Gillis did his chores he shadow boxed, training and carrying out his assignments at the same time. If he had to carry water from the spring down below the house, Teed carried the empty bucket to the spring for him. He was afraid that Gillis might hurt himself with his bucket. He knew that if the boy got cut just fighting with an empty water bucket, maybe he would be afraid of getting a cut in a real boxing match. Teed couldn't afford to let something like that happen to his young fighter. He watched over Gillis like a hen protecting her chickey-diddles.

Gillis enjoyed listening to the boxing matches on the old battery radio. When the battery was weak, he sat with his ear right against the speaker to hear the announcer call every blow that was thrown. He did not want to miss anything, even the commercials. He enjoyed hearing the Gillette jingles, the sponsor of the fights.

Teed feared that Gillis might get a cauliflower ear if a fighter should happen to throw a wild, haymaker punch. Teed didn't know what a cauliflower ear was, but he realized that it could happen to Gillis if he got hit by a big punch. Teed was young and thought things like that. He didn't want his fighter to get hurt, so he kept a close eye on Gillis' ear when the boys listened to fights.

After a big heavyweight title fight, between Joe Louis and Ezzard Charles, which Gillis had listened to on the radio, Teed gave the kid an ear check. As he gave the ears a good going-over, he noticed something that could have been the start of a dreaded cauliflower ear. After a closer scrutiny, he found it to be a small mole. He was relieved to find that it was only a nature spot.

*   *   *   *

One afternoon, as the boys and girls walked home from school, they approached the Joe-lot, a small area clear of trees. How that spot by the side of the road got its name, no one knew. Maybe it was named for some character who had lived in the area in times past.

A big grape vine—about as long as a short piece of railroad—lay stretched out in the ankle-high grass in the middle of the Joe-lot. No one knew where the grapevine came from or how it got there. There were no trees close by. Some person had put it there, of course.

Gillis made a boxing ring by placing that grapevine end-to-end in a large circle in the center of the grassy clearing. "That's a fine ring for people if they can't get along and have some differences to settle," he said, a big smile almost tearing his face apart at the seams.

"We could have a boxing tournament in that ring to weed out the weakest and worst fighters. We could have a champion right here on Coaley Creek," Teed suggested.

"That's a good idee, Teed!" Gillis agreed. "We'll have to check with ever'body at school tomorrow and see who wants to enter our fights. We can pair them according to age and size and then let them start fisticuffing to the last fight, the one where the winner takes all—all of the championship, that is."

"Who wants to try to eliminate me?" Claudette Skinner, Teed and Gillis' little cousin, asked as she jumped into the ring and hopped around like a little banty hen on a hot rock. She held her clinched fists up in front of her face and peeped through them. "Who? Who? Who?" she continued to ask, jumping up and down like someone trying to stamp out a fire. She banty-hen hopped, skipped, and jumped all around the grapevine ring and

— 83 —

shadow boxed and continued to ask, "Who? Who? Who?"

She reminded Teed of a baby hoot owl as she continued to move around and ask who dared to accept her challenge.

For a few seconds no one moved or said a word. Only Claudette moved around the ring and asked who dared to step into her domain and test her skills at defending her bragging rights.

Old fast and furious Gillis Cornfield made his entrance into the ring and commenced to stalk his adversary—Cousin Claudette Skinner. He held his fists in front of his face and peeped through them, searching for Claudette, who continued to bounce around the ring. He waited for a chance to land a telling punch to any part of his opponent's body. He had that look of a champion on his serious face.

Teed had been working with his brother on going to the body with his punches.

Thump! A sudden blow to poor little Claudette's tummy knocked the wind out of her sails. "Who? Who? Who?" ceased, and so did the foot movements that had carried the little girl around the ring while putting on a show for the bunch of boys and girls.

There stood Claudette, holding her tummy and gasping for air like a chickey-diddle with the gapes. After what seemed like forever, she finally got a breath of fresh air into her lungs and began to cry.

The bout was over with only one punch. There were no more challenges. The tournament was over. Gillis Cornfield was the reigning champion—uncrowned, of course.

Friday, Teed's sister, tried to calm Cousin Claudette by putting an arm around the convulsing little body and saying consoling words to her as everyone left the Joe-lot and headed toward the head of the hollow, paying no attention to the little girl humping and gimping along the rocky road, crying her heart out like she had lost her best friend.

Things were back to normal, or so Teed thought, after he left Cousin Claudette at her house and continued the walk home, but they weren't.

The rhododendron thicket shook as Teed's cousins, Tug and Dut, burst into the road, followed by Aunt Meg, huffing and puffing, straining every

muscle in her chubby body to keep up with her fleet-footed sons.

When Gillis heard the loud thrashing sound in the laurel thicket, he thought it might be a "haint" and was ready to do some road work. Teed's training had taken an effect on the uncrowned champ.

When Aunt Meg finally arrived—several minutes after Tug and Dut got there—where Teed, Gillis, and Friday stood waiting, she asked what was going on.

Before anyone could answer, Dut challenged Gillis to a fight to avenge his little sister's loss in the grapevine ring.

As the two combatants came together, Gillis forgot all about his training to be a boxer and clamped his teeth onto Dut's left jaw. He didn't just bite down momentarily and turn loose. He gave it a pit-bulldog clamp and held on while Dut screamed, jerked, and did a wild dance in an effort to break Gillis' tooth hold on his jaw.

Dut tried to fight back but couldn't. He had been dewclawed, it seemed. He was at a disadvantage with a set of incisors embedded in his jaw and Gillis' arms and legs wrapped around him.

Teed figured that maybe he could persuade Dut to join his boxing stable. The boy surely had a fighter's guts and instincts. Teed was so excited with his fighter's performance that he did a lot of hopping and jumping up and down. He could hardly contain himself. He was so intoxicated by the fervor of the bout that he was of little help to Aunt Meg. He could not contain his animate pleasure for the fight but was soon brought back to reality. He grabbed Gillis around the waist and began to pull like a hunter trying to pull a possum out of a hound's mouth.

It took all three—Aunt Meg, Cousin Tug, and Teed—to untangle those two combatants wrapped around each other in serious battle.

Friday had found a seat a safe distance from the fracas, and there she sat as if the fight was no big deal. She knew that it would have to end sooner or later, so she was just going to sit there and let it take its course.

"What happened to you young 'uns?" Aunt Meg asked after succeeding in parting the two boys. She gave the teeth marks on Dut's jaw a good inspection while waiting for an answer from the children.

If there had been a cavity in one of Gillis' teeth, one could have seen which had the cavity and the magnitude of it.

Dut looked as if he had been fighting with a piranha and had come in second. He had tears in his eyes, but he still wanted to have another chance to get it on with Gillis.

Teed explained to Aunt Meg what had really happened.

"Bust take it all, Teed!" Aunt Meg laughed. "If we paid attention to everything that happened amongst you kids, us grown-ups would be in a continuous war here on Coaley Creek. You all go on home now. Dut, you come with me," she said, straining to hold Cousin Dut's hand to keep him under control.

Cousin Dut still wanted another round with Gillis, and Gillis had his jaws cranked up for more action with Dut, or anyone else who felt like taking him on. He was ready for a fight and didn't care who knew it. He was ready to take on the whole world, if he had to.

Aunt Meg, Cousin Tug, and Cousin Dut went back down the road toward their house. Teed, Gillis, and Friday went toward their house at the head of the hollow, leaving an empty, silent battleground.

Teed dreaded having to face Marn. He knew that his father would find out what had happened—that the fight had taken place. He figured that Friday would be sure to tell Marn all about it. She would do it just for the fun of watching him whip smarty Teed. Teed realized that he should have stopped Gillis from fighting with little Claudette Skinner in the grapevine ring at the Joe-lot. The fight with Claudette had led to the scrap with Dut. He knew that he would be in for a double helping of hickory tea if Friday told on him. He hoped that she wouldn't.

That night Gillis hung up his gloves. The era of another boxer had ended. Well, maybe it was for the best. Gillis was only a little shaver—six years old. He would never be a punch-drunk fighter. He had thrown only one punch in his short career and had not been hit even once.

The Great Swimsuit

One day Judge L. came home with a swimsuit. No one knew where, when, why, or from whom he got the swimsuit. There was one thing for certain, though: he had a swimsuit and he was as proud as a possum with its own pokeberry patch. He was one happy boy and let everybody know it.

Judge L. put the swimsuit on to see if it would fit. Actually, it was about three sizes too large for him, but no one could tell him differently. One would think that if he had bought the swimsuit, he would have picked a size that fit. Where he got it was a mystery to everyone, and that mystery could not be solved by the rest, for Judge L. could be a very secretive person when he wanted to be.

Judge L. strutted around, posing, showing off his fine physique—if he had a physique. He must have been hiding it from the rest, for no one had seen him with one before. Judge L. was happy, and that was all that really mattered, physique or no physique.

Teed noticed that his brother was acting peculiar—nothing unusual for Judge L. He did not seem to be very comfortable while wearing his new swimsuit. Maybe he was modest or something. Or maybe he had just become aware of the fact that his swimsuit wasn't the right size. It certainly wasn't too small!

Judge L. twisted his body and scratched his hips, sides, stomach, and other parts. He did not complain very much. That was like Judge L. to a tee. He wasn't a person to complain much—ever—regardless of what it was.

Teed envied his brother. Judge L. had a swimsuit and Teed didn't. Teed knew that he shouldn't be envious of anything someone else had, but a swimsuit like the one that Judge L. possessed was one of the best reasons one could have to feel envy toward anyone.

One Sunday morning—Teed was sure that it was Sunday, since he didn't have to work that day—Judge L. approached him with a thistle-eating grin splitting his amiable face, threatening to rip his ears off.

Teed sat on the chop block in the woodyard, whittling on a cedar stick.

The Cornfields liked to whittle, and when they weren't doing anything else, they could be found whittling on a stick of some kind, and there Teed sat, just whittling away, watching the slivers of wood corkscrew their way to the thick bed of chips near his feet.

"Teed," Judge L. spoke, approaching the whittler, "how would you like to have a swimsuit?"

"What good's a new swimsuit if they ain't any water around to swim in?" Teed asked. "The only time I get wet is when I take a bath. That ain't very often in the summertime, when I can sneak in bed at night without Mom seeing me, that is. I sure wouldn't get very clean in a swimsuit if I did take one."

Teed tried not to show a lot of interest in the great swimming trunks, but deep down inside he was aching for the chance to own one just like it. He was almost drooling for a chance to accept the offered gift. He held his hand over his mouth to hide any greed that might be showing on his excited face.

"Me, Dump, Clem, Bart, and Jake are gonna dam up the creek over in the fer-field, and then you can swim with us," Judge L. invited, tempting Teed into taking the great swimsuit.

"Since you put it that way, I'll take it," Teed agreed, beaming with excitement as he accepted the swimsuit. He should have known there was something wrong about the proposal Judge L. had made. Teed had been pranked many times by his brothers, but at that very moment he was so excited that the possibility of a prank was nowhere near his mind. Judge L. would never give anything to someone without something in return. But Teed was excited and ready to barter if necessary, but it turned out that there was no reason to haggle over the matter.

Judge L. bubbled with laughter inside, but he masked his amusement fairly well. Since Teed was already blinded by the thought of receiving the swimsuit, Judge L. did not have to put forth much of an effort to hide his delight. He walked away with a big smile of triumph, and Teed was not smart enough to see that he had been tricked by his mischievous brother.

Sure enough, the older boys dammed up the little creek that meandered through the hillside farm. They made a nice swimming hole, but no one wanted to swim in it right then. There wasn't enough water and, too, it was too muddy—almost as thick as potato soup.

The swimming hole would have to fill with a volume of water deep enough to dabble in. Maybe it would clear by morning. And maybe the mud would sink back to the bottom where it belonged. Even though the muck would be stirred up once more, the water would be clear for one good swim, or dog paddle, as the boys called their swimming sessions.

Marn laughed and told the boys that they would be a bunch of water dogs, thrashing around like mud daubers. He could say some funny things relating to the boys' mode of entertainment. The boys knew that their father was just joshing them about what he said, but matter of fact he was usually right.

Teed could hardly wait for morning to come to try out his new swim-suit. Late that Sunday afternoon or early evening—about milking time—he decided to don his greatest possession and show it off for the rest of the sib-lings.

Everyone had a good, hearty, uproarious laugh as the little boy strutted about, putting on a fashion show for his audience.

The swimsuit didn't fit very well. Teed had to pull the waistband up to his armpits to tie the drawstrings. He wrapped the long string around his skinny little body a couple of times and tied it, using a granny knot. The leg area reached almost to his knobby knees. He thought that he really looked good, and he let his brothers and sisters know just how he felt about it. The swimsuit didn't fit the way he would have preferred, but he knew that he could swim much better in that swimsuit than he could with nothing on at all. Let them laugh all they wanted to. He would show them just how well he could swim in his new swimsuit come Monday morning. He would leave that bunch of jokers far behind the next day on their first swim at breakneck speed across the fifteen-foot-wide stream.

Teed had one of those brief-type swimsuits. It would have looked funny, and probably would have been much too large, had it been the boxer-type. He felt that it fit just about right. He strutted around a little for the amusement of his older brothers and sisters, and soon he began to feel just a tad uncomfortable. That swimsuit must have been made of wool, since it was so hot and scratchy. He soon realized the motive for Judge L.'s kindness and his willingness to part with his prized possession. Teed should have known there was a catch somewhere in that swap that involved only one item.

That wily Judge L. had almost forced Teed to take the swimsuit. He had led the boy on by telling him what a fine garment it was and how much fun he could have while swimming in it. Since Teed was just a little shaver, Judge L. could manipulate him any way he wished.

Whenever one of the kids got something new, the first thing he did was show it to Marn.

Teed decided to show his father the new swimsuit. Away he skipped, itching and scratching as he went. He saw Marn at the barn, scattering shelled corn on the ground for the chickens, so he ran in that direction. He skipped along, itching and scratching more often since the sun bore down on him, causing him to perspire profusely under the scratchy swimsuit.

A hula dancer could have learned a few good moves watching Teed as he twisted and scratched. Even though he was uncomfortable, he was so happy that he felt as if he owned the world and everyone owed him rent, due that day.

Teed heard a noise behind him, and when he turned to see what caused the commotion, he saw that it was Old Horny, the cow. She shook her head and brandished a pair of huge horns as she followed Teed. The little boy ran as fast as he could toward the barn and his father. He hotfooted it along, but when he looked back, not from curiosity but from fear, he saw that he was losing the race.

Old Horny was gaining fast and would soon overtake Teed—then what? He couldn't afford to let that happen, for he might get dirt, and maybe some blood, on his new swimsuit. He didn't want that to happen. He wanted his swimsuit to stay clean so he could be ready to jump into the swimming hole without having to wait for it to dry, so he tried to turn up the speed another notch or two.

The little fellow reached back for a handful of reserved energy to help him in the race for his life but found no reserves. He was using his very last surge of power right then. He needed help! He couldn't call for anyone to come to his rescue. He needed all his strength and breath to run on right then. As he sped toward the corncrib, he spied a sled with a deep wooden box on it. Into that sled box he dived. It was no swan dive, mind you. He wasn't worried about his diving form—just his form in general. Old Horny could change his physical appearance if she succeeded in chasing the little boy down.

Teed lay in the bottom of the sled—his eyes closed—and screamed at the top of his lungs. When he finally looked up, there stood the cow looking down at him, a greedy expression on her ordinarily docile face. Old Horney couldn't reach her horns to the bottom of the box and gore the boy, but that didn't make things any less serious for Teed.

The cow stood there, looking down in the sled with those big soft eyes never blinking. There was a serious look on that cow's face.

Teed knew that Old Horney could gulp him down, right after she finished dicing and pureeing him with her long, sharp horns. The next time he could garner enough courage to open his eyes to survey the dilemma, there stood Judge L., laughing.

Judge L. was laughing harder than Teed had ever heard his brother laugh; harder even than Bart laughed when he told Judge L. to stop the humongous wagon by grabbing the rear wheels. Tears streamed down Judge L.'s cheeks. Convulsive laughter continued to wrack his skinny body.

Teed was sure that Judge L. had saved his life. He continued to yell, though, unaware of what he was doing at the moment.

"What's wrong with that boy?" Marn asked, arriving at the scene of all the action and looking down into the sled box at Teed.

Teed couldn't see Marn from his position in the bottom of the sled— he had his eyes closed—but just to hear his voice gave the kid courage. He slowly opened his eyes, raised up, and looked around to see where the cow was. She had gone to the barn.

Judge L. could hardly talk for laughing and hiccuping, trying to tell his father what had happened. "Teed was practicing for the Olympics," he giggled. "The cow was helping in his training. She was helping him build up his muscles and lungs. Now Teed can swim in the Olympics. He has his swimsuit and he's been training by running. I think he's ready to take on the entire world. Ever'body had better watch out. He's ready and raring to go right now."

"That crazy cow tried to horn me!" Teed told Marn. He lay back down on the bottom of the sled, still afraid to rise above the protective sides, even though Marn and Judge L. were there where they could defend him from further attack by the cow.

"Ol' Horny thought Teed was a cornstalk," Marn laughed. "She was just trying to catch him so she could have a good supper. She must have been real hungry to run fast enough to tree Teed in the sled box."

There was a lot of laughing going on, but Teed did not think it was funny. How could they laugh at such a serious thing as he faced—those two big horns on that old cow's head.

"I've just got to go tell Dump and the others," Judge L. said, running toward the house. He could not hold the humor he saw in the incident. He had to share it with someone else before he burst from trying to hold it all bottled up in his laughing box.

The family had a good laugh, as usual.

Bart rolled on the floor, laughing so hard that he lost his breath and began to heave like a sick dog.

One member of the family could get scared, as Teed had, or get hurt, as he could have been, and everyone would guffaw about it.

At the supper table that night, Marn informed everyone that the corn had to be hoed for the last time—"laid by" as they called the last hoeing.

"Oh, no!" Teed whined. "I was hoping that we could go swimming tomorrow. The creek should rise a lot, maybe to the top of the dam."

"You can swim after we finish hoeing the corn," Marn told him.

Teed had nothing else to say since Marn had made his decision. No matter how much Teed might whine, Marn had already decided what was scheduled for the morrow.

*　*　*　*

Monday morning came too quickly. It seemed to Teed that he had just closed his eyes to sleep and then his mother shook him awake. The morning meal wasn't very exciting to him, only stomach filling. He finished eating and then rose with the rest of his brothers and sisters, who were joking and laughing, as usual. Teed walked as slow as possible—as slow as he could get by with—until his father put a little fire under his feet. He stepped a little faster and caught up with the rest, then took his place in the row above Judge L. for the first trip through the field.

That field of corn was pure torture, and it was all Teed's fault. He wanted to be the first one in the swimming hole, so he wore his nice but scratchy swimsuit under his bibbed overalls. As time passed, Teed became more uncomfortable as the sun bore down on his wool swimsuit.

Marn had to remind Teed often to get back to hoeing corn. "You can do your scratching later," he stated sternly, letting Teed know who was in charge.

Teed could not keep from scratching. The scratching just had to be done, or else he would surely die. He would hoe a hill or two, then stop to scratch his bottom. The heat was killing him dead in his tracks. He couldn't wait until they finished hoeing that big field of corn before he could get relief.

Finally work for the day ended, and everyone ran toward the swimming hole—the younger ones did.

Dump took the horse to the barn, unharnessed him, and released him to wallow in the dusty barnyard, while Clem put the double-shovel plow in the toolshed behind the barn, which made them just a tad late getting to the swimming hole.

Teed had one of the galluses of his bibbed overalls unbuttoned, ready to slip them off as soon as he reached the swimming hole. He was so excited! He would be the first one to hit the water.

Bart, Jake, and Judge L. arrived at the swimming hole first. They could run much faster than Teed, but they had to undress and put on cut-offs to swim in. One planned to skinny-dip—Bart, of course. Anyone could have guessed that.

Teed dropped his overalls. There he stood in his fine swimsuit. "The last one in's a rotten egg and stinks worse!" he yelled. He ran to be first in the water and dived over the edge of the bank. He went down, down, down for what seemed like a short eternity. Finally, he hit smack-dab in the middle of the creek, but there was no water. His head had buried up to his chin in the slimy mud on the bottom of the empty swimming hole. The oozy mess covered his head and gushed up his nose. He gagged and spat several times, trying to rid his mouth of the mud in order to yell for help.

Finally, Teed was able to disengage his head from the muddy prison—no help from the rest of the group. What a relief! He doubted if any of the other boys would have helped him quickly. He figured that they were about to die laughing at him right then. Sure enough, as he pulled his head out of the mud, he heard the others laughing. Bart was laughing the hardest of all.

Teed walked up the creek in search of a pool with enough water in it to wash the mud out of his hair, nose, and ears. Unable to find a good place to wash up, he went to the house to ask his mother to wash his dirty head for him.

The dam had broken during the night, letting all the water leak out. That did not curb the lads' enthusiasm. They commenced to build a new dam—like a bunch of beavers. They replaced boards and daubed cracks with hair-grass sods dug from the edge of the creek.

* * * *

Marn smiled at Teed. "Your head looks like a mud dauber's nest with all that mud in it," he said.

Teed held his hands over his eyes to keep the lye soap from getting in them while Vann washed the creek mud from his hair. He hoped that she would finish quickly so he could hurry back to help rebuild the swimming-hole dam.

"Be sure the swimming hole is full of water before you dive in," Marn told Teed, smiling at the little boy's muddy head in the washbasin.

"I will, Dad," Teed promised, wincing as Vann scrubbed a little too hard in her efforts to remove the mud.

Grillers, 'Nanners, and Chickey-diddles

There were very few toys or other forms of entertainment for the Cornfield children. There wasn't enough outside income to make such things affordable.

As Teed grew up on Coaley Creek, he had to do without store-bought toys. If he couldn't make his own toys, he just had to do without them.

Entertainment consisted of ordinary physical games and an old battery radio, when the battery was new. There was also an occasional picture show, if the older brothers and sisters had enough money and took the time to take the little squirts, as they called Teed and Gillis, along for a day of pure bliss in the movie theater at Big Onion Gap—five long miles from the Cornfields' house.

The older children had taken in a movie—or "show," as they called it—a thrill-packed, shoot-'em-up cowboy western on a Saturday afternoon. The theater marquee had it listed as a matinee. The Cornfields did not care what it was called. They enjoyed it, whatever it was.

Judge L. related the exciting movie to Teed and Gillis.

A rancher captured a gorilla in the jungle and brought it back with him to the United States to his big cattle ranch, somewhere near a Texas town. The rancher taught the gorilla to do things for him so he would not have to work so hard.

Teed and Gillis liked the story. They had never seen a gorilla in a movie before. They had not seen one alive, either. How they wished that they could have seen that good show.

"You ain't lying to us about that griller, are you, Judge L.?" Gillis said, his big brown eyes bulging and snapping with excitement. "That griller could really do all them things that you said it could do? Are you sure that you ain't just joshin' me and Teed about all of this, making out that you've seen a griller that could do all kinds of things like that? What you're tellin' us is hard to believe."

"Yeah, I'm telling the honest-to-goodness truth; it sure could do all them things, and more, too," Judge L. told him. "And I ain't joshing you. I'm telling you the truth. So, if you want to hear the story about the griller, just shut up and listen. I can't tell it good if you keep buttin' in all the time."

"What else more could it do?" Gillis asked, getting as close to Judge L. as he could to listen to the details of the good gorilla story.

"Well, it could saddle the man's horse and bring it to him to ride to town and back," Judge L. explained.

"Now, you can't make me believe that a griller can do things like people," Teed said. "How long did the man have the griller before he could get it to do what he wanted it to? It would take a long, long time to teach an animal to do fetching and stuff like that. Ol' Bowser will fetch a ball back to me sometimes, but I know that he can't put a saddle on Ol' Jock and fetch him out of the barn for me to ride up to Big Onion Gap and back."

"Daddy and Mommy wouldn't let you go all the way to Big Onion Gap and back by yourself, Teed," Gillis argued.

"I was just using that as an example," Teed came back. "I'm big enough to ride to Big Onion Gap and back if I wanted to. I don't want to is all there is to it. Now, as I was saying about Ol' Bowser, he'd be an old dog dead before he could learn as much as that griller did. How do you know that it wasn't just a man dressed up in a griller suit, Judge L.?"

"'Cause they would have to catch a griller and skin it's hide off of it to make a man a griller suit," Gillis blurted out before Judge L. could respond to the question. "Nobody would kill a live griller to make a suit out of it just for a man to wear one time in a show. It would be crazy for someone to kill the griller when he could train the griller to do his work for him. You must be making all this stuff up just to josh us around."

"It was a real griller, boys. I tell it for a fact," Judge L. avowed. "It would jump up and down, making funny, excited noises as if it was expecting payment for the work it had done for the man."

"Did the man give it a dime to pay it for doing the work for him?" Gillis asked.

"No, dummy," Teed quipped. "I know that much. You should know that a griller couldn't go to the store and spend its dime." Teed could not understand why his little brother thought that a gorilla could spend money and know correct change. "Anyone should know that a store clerk wouldn't give change to a monkey."

"He was waiting for a 'nanner as his pay," Judge L. continued. "He wasn't waiting for change. But it could spend money. The rancher sent the griller to the grocery store with some money and a list of things that he wanted, and the griller went right on down to the store, right in the middle of the town, and got what was on the list, paid for it, and brought it back home, just as big as you please."

"Did the griller read the list and add 'nanners and goodies to it for hisself?" Teed wanted to know. "If he knew enough to pay for ever'thing," he went on, "then he knew enough to get what he wanted."

"You know that a griller can't write or read," Gillis said. "He probably just picked out what he wanted and paid for it with the change that he got back when he paid for the man's stuff."

"You boys are getting things wrong," Judge L. said. "He was an exceptionally smart griller. He couldn't add and read or give back change, but he was smart in ever' other way you could think of. He was trained, not taught smarts like from a book. He didn't go to go to a public school to learn things."

"You said that he was waiting to be paid for his work," Teed said. "I still say that it was a man dressed up like a griller, acting silly like a griller."

"No, it wasn't a man dressed up like a griller doing all them things," Judge L. snapped. "He was just as smart as a man is all. When the man give him a 'nanner, he peeled it and eat it up. He was real smart. No man would take a 'nanner for his pay. The men that worked on the ranch in the show used their money at the saloon. Single men did, but the married men just took their pay home and gave it to their wives to spend any way the women wanted to. The cowboys got to go to the saloon anyway. I guess their wives gave them an allowance out of their pay, or something like that. You boys would have to see the show in order to understand what really went on. I can only tell you, and if you don't believe me, then that's your own fault, and I can't help it."

"The griller should have traded his 'nanner for a drink at the saloon like the men did," Gillis said.

"Grillers don't drink alcohol or beer," Judge L. groaned. "Just Griller Joe went to town and to all the saloons—not the griller."

"Who was Griller Joe?" Teed wanted to know. "Was he the griller or just a man dressed up like a griller, like I said before?"

"Teed, you don't know anything at all," Judge L. said, glaring at him. "Griller Joe was the rancher that owned the griller. The griller's name was Varoom."

"That sure is a crazy name," Gillis laughed. "That sounds like somebody pouring on the gas in a big truck." He ran around the yard. "Varoom! Varoom! Varoom!" he roared, digging his little feet into the grass and dirt, imitating the spinning of a truck's wheels.

Gillis liked big trucks. He hoped that someday he could be a truck driver and go on long hauls in a big red diesel rig. He had a great desire to get behind the wheel of a big truck and let the wind blow in his face as he raced along the highway.

"From now on I ain't gonna tell you two kids about the shows that I see!" Judge L. stormed. "You two ain't mature enough to understand about what can be done in a picture show. They've got a whole lot of animals that's trained to work in all kinds of shows. Just wait till you're old enough to start going to the show real often and want to tell me about it. I won't believe anything that you tell me. Not even if it is true."

"Give Judge L. a 'nanner, Gillis," Teed suggested. "Maybe he's just hungry and thinking out of his head. Maybe a 'nanner will bring him back to his senses, and then he can tell us what really happened in the show that he saw about that griller that is as smart as a man."

Gillis handed Judge L. a corncob that he found lying by the yard fence.

"I ought to rub your head with this cob," Judge L. said, chasing Gillis around the house.

"Mommy! Mommy! Mommy!" Gillis screamed, running for the

kitchen. "Judge L. is gonna cob me!" he shouted, rushing through the door to the safety of the kitchen. Judge L. ended the chase and went in search of the older brothers and sisters—somewhere at an unknown location on the farm. He started yelling, but received no answer. When he received no answer the first time, he yelled again. "Hey, ever'body! Where in the cat hair are you?"

After Judge L. left in search of his older brothers, Gillis came back outside and joined Teed. The boys resumed playing their favorite games. They had just started a good game of trucks, using empty meat cans as their trucks, when their mother called from the kitchen.

"Hey, Teed and Gillis, I want you all to go and gather some eggs for me. I'm going to make a stack cake for Sunday's after-meetin' dinner," she told them. She fanned her face with her apron while standing in the doorway, where a faint breeze entered the hot room.

"We'll do it, Mom," Teed called in answer to her request. He threw his empty meat-can truck under the floor of the house and headed toward the henhouse, with Gillis following behind, still carrying his meat can.

"Get rid of that meat can, Gillis," Teed said. "You might fall on it and cut your hand plum' off."

Gillis threw the meat can under a snowball bush by the fence and followed Teed toward the henhouse situated about a hundred yards below the dwelling house.

The boys followed a path between two thickets of briars and elderberry bushes.

That part of the farm was too rocky to use for a garden, so the briars and elderberry bushes were at home among the rocks. The brush was cut once a year, usually during the summer. The older boys enjoyed cutting the briars and bushes so they could search for snakes.

Teed had heard his father say that copperheads were as thick as flies in those thickets and rocks. There were several copperheads killed each time the bushes and briars were cut.

There were no eggs in the henhouse, so Teed and Gillis went on toward the barn that sat on the only flat spot in the side of the steep hill.

Teed talked incessantly about owning a gorilla just like the one in the movie.

"If we had a griller like the one in the show, we could teach it to work, then we could play," Gillis said.

"He sure would be a lot of help," Teed agreed, daydreaming of having a gorilla to do his work so he could be free to play and do the many things he enjoyed the most.

A small stream meandered through the swampy barnyard. As the boys came to the stream, Teed splashed water on Gillis and ran up the hill, starting a chase.

By the time Gillis caught up with Teed, he had forgotten about the splashing he had received.

There were no eggs in the barn, so the boys went on toward a tree stump near the barn. Teed had found a hen's nest there a few days earlier. He hoped that the hen was still using the stump as a nest. There were three fresh eggs lying in the leaves at the bottom of the stump, letting Teed know that the hen had not given up her hidden nest, although Teed had taken all of her eggs away from her the day he found them.

Teed sat down on the edge of the stump to rest. "What if a griller lived in our barn, Gillis?" he wondered. He was still thinking of the movie that Judge L. had seen. He couldn't get it off his mind.

"The horses wouldn't like that," Gillis said. "Let's take the eggs to Mom so she can make a cake for Sunday dinner. I'd like to sop the batter bowl."

"I can't understand how you can like raw cake batter, Gillis," Teed grimaced, shaking his head and making a puckered face.

"That should be easy to understand, Teed," Gillis replied. "It tastes good is why I can like it."

"Let's play a game, Gillis," Teed suggested. "We can take the eggs to the house later."

"We'd better take 'em right on to the house. Mom'll bust our hides if we don't," Gillis warned.

"She won't," Teed laughed. "You know she won't. She might fuss at us a little, but she won't bust our hides, like you say. Come on." He walked toward the barn. "I'll be a big griller, and you can be the owner like in the show."

"Why can't I be the griller?" Gillis asked, whining in protest.

"Because I'm going to be the griller, Gillis," Teed replied. "I'm bigger then you are. Grillers ain't little like you. Do you remember how big Judge L. said that show griller was? You can't saddle a horse, so you can't be a big griller."

"You can't saddle a horse, either, Teed," Gillis argued.

"But I'm much bigger than you are, so I'll be the griller," Teed declared. "Tell me to get you something from the store and give me some money to pay for it. I'll go get what you want and bring back your change. I might get something special, so give me plenty of money."

"If you get anything that's special, you'll have to charge it. I don't have any money," Gillis said, just as somber as could be.

"It's make-believe money, Gillis," Teed chuckled. "So you can give me a whole bushel of make-believe money, can't you?"

"Sure! I can handle that, Teed," he said. "Here, take a zillion dollars and forget about the change." He held his hands out as far apart as he could reach, indicating that he had a huge bundle of money.

Teed pretended to take the money and cram it into his pockets.

"A griller don't have pockets, Teed!" Gillis said.

"This one does," Teed insisted, simulating the act of stuffing the imaginary money into his pockets. "Now, what do you want me to go to the store and get for you?"

Just then, a hen and a bunch of chickey-diddles went past—the hen clucking, the chickey-diddles peeping.

"Let's pretend that them chickey-diddles are dodo birds that was here before people got created," Teed suggested. "They was here millions of years ago but ain't here no more. They all got killed off or the dinosaurs ate 'em up or something like that."

"Who wants a bird a zillion years old?" Gillis asked. "He'd be too tough. I want something tender, so I want a little, tender chickey-diddle. Get me a chickey-diddle, Varoom."

"No, I'm not Varoom like in the show, Gillis," Teed said. "Just call me Vic."

"Why change the name from Varoom to Vic?" Gillis wanted to know. "Don't you think that's an odd name for a griller?"

"How many grillers do you know, Gillis?" Teed queried.

"None," Gillis came back.

"Well, Vic ain't an odd name for a griller then," Teed said.

"Get me a tough dodo bird a zillion years old, Vic," Gillis ordered.

Teed got down on his hands and knees and began chasing the chickey-diddles in an effort to separate one from the hen. He succeeded in his quest, and when he was about ready to pounce on it, he was hit from behind.

That old setting hen began to flog, scratch, peck, and beat him with her wings. Teed was more scared than hurt. He began to scream and ran down the hill toward the house. The eggs in the tree stump were forgotten. He had been attacked by a monster!

"It's just a hen!" Gillis laughed. "It ain't nary monster or booger. Stop and fight it. You're a griller, and a griller is bigger than a hen, even bigger than a booger is." He continued to chide Teed bravely until the hen turned on him. As fear gripped the little fellow, he began to scream. He ran down the hill, trying to catch up with Teed.

Marn was at the crib shelling a turn of corn for a trip to the gristmill at Jestus Branch to have it ground into meal for bread. When he heard the commotion on the hill, he came outside the building to investigate the cause.

"What's wrong, Teed?" he asked as the little boys ran at breakneck speed down the yellow clay bank. "Why are you crying?"

"We was playing griller and chasing dodo birds when a hen flogged me," Teed answered, continuing to run and cry.

"What's wrong with *you*, Gillis?" Marn asked.

"A hen flogged Teed," he cried, running on after Teed.

Marn could see the hen gathering her scattered chickey-diddles back together up there above the barn. He knew that the boys wouldn't bother that hen and her chicks again.

Coaley Creek Treasure

The Cornfield children had always wanted to find a humongous treasure and dig it up. The chance to get rich had always eluded them, even though they had searched long and hard to find treasures to dig up and turn into cash money. They hoped to change their lifestyle from one of struggling with tough times and money worries to one of leisure and luxury.

Jake and Judge L. found a hidden treasure—they figured—hidden beneath a stand of trees on the mountain, just below Isome Gap, but free time to put to digging it up had not come around. That free time finally came one day—one beautiful Sunday morning—and the duo decided to get into the job that they had postponed so many times before. They were ready to become rich folks for a change. The boys had talked about it all summer, ever since they had discovered it in the early spring.

The Cornfields had a big crop of corn, oats, and hay, plus the two big vegetable gardens to tend to during the summer. Sundays were the only days of rest that the boys had during those weeks of summer vacation from school. They had chores to do on Sunday, but they usually spent the remainder of that day of rest playing a few games and riding wooden-wheeled wagons down the yellow clay bank over near the milk gap.

The yellow bank had a gully in it which was about three feet wide at the top, tapering to one foot wide in the bottom at a depth of two feet. That gully made riding wooden-wheeled wagons a humongous challenge. There was no way to ride out of the trench that nature had cut during the times of heavy runoff of water from falling rains and the melting snows of the many years in the past. The trench was too wide for the wagon wheels to straddle it, since the normal width of a wagon was about two feet. There was a rut cut in each side of the gully, about a foot below the top, where the wagon wheels made their marks as they rolled to the bottom of the hill.

Occasionally there was a crash of a wagon as one of the wagoners dared to ride his wagon at an angle down the hill, putting one set of wheels in the center of the gully and letting the opposite side follow the angled contour of the course. One had to be a good wagon master to conquer a course like that.

Many hours were filled with that type of banter, followed by a few days of less bravery due to sore body parts caused by the bumps and bruises sustained by tumbling about with an upended wagon.

Since there was a lull in the work program—the hay was cut and stored, oats cradled, tied, and stored, and the corn laid by—Jake and Judge L. decided to dig up the big treasure and end their working days—permanently. There would no longer be any reason to work after the treasure was turned into cash.

They had planned the digging numerous times, but their plans had been altered each time. They had not changed plans voluntarily. Work and chores had been the lurking culprits that put a kink in their quest for an easy fortune.

"We've put this digging off much too long," Jake said as he walked along the path with Judge L.

"That's a real fact," Judge L. agreed. "We should have dug it up as soon as we found it—or when Esker Seedy and Cousin Jubal found it. Them's awful good boys to share their treasure with us. They don't have to share with us to be our good friends, do they?"

"No. But it sure helps," Jake grinned.

The two boys were on their way to the blacksmith shop that sat under a huge beech tree near the hog-lot to get a shovel and a mattock to dig the dirt and shovel it away to find the buried treasure.

"I guess we'd better get a crowbar to move the big rocks with," Jake suggested.

"Naw, we won't need a crowbar," Judge L. replied. "We can move the three marker rocks by hand—just roll them away. They're all the rocks that're around there. Soft dirt's all that'll be left, I'd say."

"I kind of doubt that. I'd say that the ground's chocked plum' full of rocks over there," Jake reflected.

"I bet the treasure hider had to carry the rocks up the hill to that location where he planted the four trees about a hundred years ago," Judge L. said.

"Those trees can't be a hundred years old," Jake stated. "They ain't big enough to be that old. They ain't more'n a foot through at the butt. I know that trees grow faster than that."

"Not in that yeller dirt on the south side of the hill," Judge L. argued. "The dirt's right over coal, and the coal takes all the growing strength away from the trees."

"I'll bet you that bee-course I found against the Christmas present that you're gonna get this year that we hit a rock the first lick that we dig in that spot," Jake predicted.

"I'm not giving up my Christmas present for a bee-course!" Judge L. retorted. "How do you know that there are any bees around that place where you say that you found them watering?"

"I saw them flying from the creek toward Isome Gap," Jake replied.

"They could be Grandpa's bees. He's probably got a hundred bee gums on his farm," Judge L. guessed.

"Naw, they ain't Grandpa's bees. They didn't look like any of Grandpa's bees—none that I'm acquainted with anyway," Jake vowed. "That bee tree's around there somewhere, just waiting for me to stumble on its location."

"What do you mean, 'none that you're acquainted with'?" Judge L. asked, facing Jake. "All bees look alike. You couldn't distinguish one bee from another, even in one bee gum, much less recognizing that one bee in a hundred bee gums full of bees just like it. You can't make me believe that you're a bee specialist. I've seen as many bees as you have, and I can't tell which gum one has come out of if I see it down at the creek getting a bellyful of water or on a flower getting nectar to make its honey out of."

"Bees don't use water to make honey," Jake said. "You sure don't know much about bees and making honey."

"You don't either," Judge L. snapped. "You're just guessing about how bees use water for honey. I say that they get the nectar out of the flowers and mix it with water and stir it up until it turns into thick honey. You can have that bee-course. They would be too hard to round up and put in a bee gum."

"You won't have to round them up—just look for them in a tree," Jake told him.

"No bet, Brother," Judge L. stated. "A Christmas present is a sure thing, and a course to a bee tree is a gamble that I won't take. But I'm sure that there ain't many rocks in the area where we intend to dig for the treasure. Just forget about a crowbar."

The two brothers, placing their tools on their shoulders, left the blacksmith shop on their way to Isome Gap and a fortune. They walked along in silence for a while.

"Is Esker Seedy and Cousin Jubal going to meet us there to help dig?" Jake asked, breaking a long silence. "They should be there. They found the treasure, you know."

"They told me faithfully that they would be there," Judge L. said. "They'll probably get lost, though. You know how they are. Them two boys would get lost in a one-seater toilet."

"Do you know where the digging place is? Did they ever show you where it's actual location is?" Jake queried.

"Sure," Judge L. responded. "I put some brash over the rocks so that they couldn't be seen by anyone, and I chopped on the trees to make them look used. People won't be suspicious of a treasure buried under the brash."

"Hey that's real smart of you to put that brash over the treasure site. I guess you're right there," Jake agreed. "Nobody would think that there's a treasure buried right under their nose."

The two lads talked about many things as they made their way to the treasure site, returning often to the subject of treasure and what they would buy with the money when it was cashed in.

"You didn't tell Teed that we planned to dig today, did you?" Jake wanted to know as he threw a rock into the woods beside the path. He watched it strike a small sapling, dead center.

"No, sir, I didn't," Judge L. assured his brother. "I didn't want any snot-nosed kids along in the way. He still wants to buy everything that I plan to buy. I told him that he don't have any money, but that don't phase him at all. He thinks that I'm gonna give him part of my share. If he thinks that I'm gonna do a crazy thing like that, he's gonna be disappointed." He threw a rock at the same tree that Jake had hit. His rock flew in a straight line and struck the bole of the tree about an inch from Jake's mark.

"I'm gonna buy Dad a big farm and a new tractor with my part," Jake said soberly. "Dad tries so hard, but with all of our mouths to fill, it's hard for him to make enough to keep us going. He deserves more than he has. With this big treasure we're going to bring in, maybe he won't have to work at all. I'd just like to see him do a lot of fishing and hunting, just for the pleasure, not for the necessity. There is one thing for sure, though: it's gonna be nice not having to work all the time."

"Yeah, you're right. It sure is gonna be real nice," Judge L. said, dreaming of a good, easy life ahead. He was brought back to reality as he and Jake turned a bend in the snake-crooked road. "Hey, there's Cousin Jubal and Esker Seedy. How're you boys doing this fine morning?" he asked his friends sitting on a big rock by the side of the road.

"If I felt any better, I don't know if I could stand it or not," Esker Seedy replied, returning the greeting.

"Yeah, I'm fine as Aunt Gussie's garter," Cousin Jubal said, sniffing loudly. Sniffing was a natural act for him. One could always tell when Cousin Jubal was in a crowd—even after dark—because of that ever-present sniffing.

"I'm doing fine, too," Tester Seedy greeted, emerging from behind a huge white oak tree, buttoning his overalls as he walked toward his friends.

"What are you doing here, Tester?" Jake asked. "Esker," he said, turning to his friend, "we weren't supposed to bring any snot-noses along. I left Teed at home, and here you brought Tester. He'll just be right in the way and could get hurt bad. Don't let him get underfoot. He can't share in the treasure, either. He's too little. He wouldn't know how to spend his share if we gave him some of it. I sure ain't givin' him any of mine, and that's a fact."

"Don't worry your pretty head, Jake," Esker said. "He's a tough little worker. He'll do just as much work as you and Judge L. put together. Besides, he helped me and Cousin Jubal find this treasure site."

"Yeah, and what do you mean by not having a snot-nosed kid along?" Tester asked. "What do you call that standing behind you, Jake? He ain't no dry-nosed kid."

Everyone looked behind Jake, where Cousin Jubal stood, sniffing and grinning all over the place.

"I think you're away off base when you think that Tester can do as much work as me and Judge L. put together," Jake said, looking hard at Esker. "But that don't matter any at all. He can help all he wants to, as long as he don't get underfoot, but he can't share the hard-earned treasure with me. You'll have to divvy up some of your part."

"I'll share with him. Just don't you worry about it," Esker stated. "We can't stay all day, though. Mommy said that we have to be home early enough to do some work for her. She don't know that I brought Tester with me. She might whip me for it when we get back over there to the house this evening."

"Yeah, Mommy will whip me and you when we get over there," Tester sang to his brother, dancing an accompanying jig in the dusty path. The rest of the boys joined his singing of the new tune.

"Mommy will whip me and you when we get over there," Jake sang. "That's a good song. If Clem was along he'd serenade us all day long with that song. He'd add more words to it, though, Tester. Now, let's get to the treasure site and commence to get rich."

"We looked for the place while we waited for you slowpokes, but we couldn't find it," Cousin Jubal said, getting into the conversation after he had sniffed several time to get cranked up in order to speak.

"Yeah, me and Tester thought maybe we had just dreamt that we found a treasure. I've dreamt of finding more'n I've found in real life," Esker declared.

"Yeah, the place ain't there," Tester stated. "I don't 'member of being in a dream with you boys. I don't even dream about anything, and I know that I never dreamt of finding treasure with you fellers."

"You sure ain't been in any of my dreams, Tester Seedy!" Judge L. exclaimed. "I can dream of a lot better things than you."

"Yeah, you could dream of his sister, Zel," Cousin Jubal laughed, then sniffed.

"Man, no, not that ugly thing!" Judge L. replied. "Anyway, she's Teed's girl."

"I wouldn't make that accusation to Teed's face," Jake warned. "You know how he hates Zel Seedy."

"I sure wouldn't 'cuse Teed of claiming my sister," Tester said. "He's busted my mouth several times for things that ain't even that bad, and I know that I could lose some of my front teeth if I went that far."

"Judge L. said that he cut some brash and piled it over the odd-shaped rocks," Jake said, changing the subject. "He covered the rocks so they wouldn't stand out as an advertisement of any hidden treasure. You chopped on the trees, too, didn't you, Judge L.?"

"Yeah, and I did a good job, too, 'cause even Esker couldn't find the camouflaged place, and he was the first person to notice that the place looked suspicious of being treasure-laden." Judge L. boasted.

"Hey, Esker, that was what we saw up there on the hill when we hunted for the place," Tester said, realizing the reason for the brush-pile on the hill.

"I guess that's why we couldn't find it," Esker supposed. "Judge L. sure is a good camouflager!"

"Esker told me that a beaver had been gnawing on the trees and that that brash pile was its lodge," Tester said, looking at his brother. "You're some crazy kid, Esker! There ain't any beavers in this part of the world. They're just in books is all."

"Well, let's go on up there and get to digging," Jake suggested. "Just standing and arguing won't make us one bit richer."

"Yeah, we're gonna have to hurry. Mommy said for us to get back early," Esker said.

"Yeah, Mommy will whip me and you when we get over there," Tester sang as he jumped up and down in the narrow path.

Jake and the rest joined in, singing the one-line song that had already made a hit with them.

The boys sang the song over and over, never tiring of the lyrics or unwritten music. They sang while they walked up the steep, rocky slope.

Up until then, Cousin Jubal had been rather quiet, and that was unusual for him. If he wasn't talking continuously, he was sniffing obnoxiously. He had to be talking or making some type of noise all the time. "When I cash in my part of that big treasure, I'm gonna buy some sheet copper and make me a good 'still," Cousin Jubal said. "I could make a lot of money, too, selling my 'shine. I allus wanted to have my own 'still."

"You won't need money or anything when we dig up that treasure, Cousin Jubal," Judge L. told him. "You'll have all the money and things that you'll ever need, and then some left over to give to your family."

"Yeah, I guess you're right there, Judge L., but I allus wanted a 'still. Copper's so bright and shiny and pretty," Cousin Jubal said.

"Yeah, it's pretty and shiny until you put a wood fire under it, then you have a black pot," Jake said. "You could set up a black coal bucket and look at it. It would do you just as much good, since you're just a tad too young to use a 'still if you had one."

"I know it, Jake, but I want a copper pot 'stead of a coal bucket," Jubal replied. "A coal bucket's too black for me."

"About like our treasure's gonna be if we don't get it dug up," Judge L. stated. "You know how hog-dollars and gold coins will tarnish when they're covered up in a hole for a long time. I'll bet those gold coins are already black with tarnish, and us standing here will let them get even blacker than they already are. They'll look like dirt, and we won't be able to distinguish between the coins and the black ground when we dig into them. We could lose a fortune by standing around here. Let's shake a leg and get to digging. Interest alone on our future bank accounts will be enough for us and our families to live on. Boy, won't that be great!"

"Yeah, it sure will be great to be rich," Esker Seedy spoke up. "I don't know," he continued, "how silver and gold will tarnish. I don't even have a penny to bury in a hole to see how long it'll take for it to turn black."

"Let's get to work," Jake ordered as they reached their destination. He began to move the brush from the treasure's marker rocks.

The boys went at their work with a fervor, with Judge L. Cornfield moving the first rock from its until-then undisturbed place in the triangular formation. He rolled it down the steep slope. The other boys stopped their work and watched as the rolling rock came to rest against a huge moss-covered boulder.

"Hey, that was great!" Cousin Jubal shouted, then picked up a flat rock and rolled it down the hill.

The boys watched Cousin Jubal's rolling rock until it stopped beside the one that Judge L. had rolled down the grade.

Judge L. had started a rock-rolling game, with the rest joining him, rolling more stones down the hill to a big boulder, where a new rock pile was taking shape.

"Look how loose the dirt is around these rocks," Jake said. "It looks like they were placed here by hand not long ago, by somebody instead of nature."

"Somebody did place them here," Judge L. stated, turning to Jake. "The man that hid the treasure under them, he's the one that placed them here like they are."

"It looks like somebody put these rocks here, and it ain't been a hundred years as you boys claim," Jake replied, looking closely at the loosely piled stones.

"It's been a long time, but rocks won't shrink down like a pile of loose dirt will," Judge L. said, continuing to roll more rocks down the hill while arguing with Jake."

"I've been dreading digging in this place," Esker Seedy said, admitting that he was just a tad lazy. "It's gonna be a lot easier than I figured it'd be, though. Look how this treasure site is in a pile of rocks, just the right size to be able to lift without bustin' a gut doing it. There ain't enough dirt in these rocks for us to have to use the shovel. It won't take us long at all to get to the treasure. That'll be to our advantage, Tester. You know we've got to get back home early this evenin.'"

"Yeah, Mommy will whip me and you when we get over there," Tester sang, and everyone joined him in song.

"The man who hid this treasure was lazy," Jake told the others. "He wanted it to be easy to get to—without a lot of work."

"Yeah, and I'm real glad he made it easy for us," Judge L. said, heaving a jagged rock down the hill. He did not watch it bounce along, banging against trees as it went, stopping before it reached the growing pile. Judge L. was too engrossed in his work and thoughts of the treasure that was so close at hand, he hoped, to watch the rock.

The walls of the hole were shored up with evenly placed rocks, like the walls of a hand-dug well. Someone had taken great pains in placing the rocks just right.

Judge L. moved another rock. "I've found something, boys!" he yelled. Judge L. happened to be the lucky treasure hunter in the pit at that very moment. He had found the treasure. "It's in a brown paper poke," he beamed, bending over to lift the bag from its resting place between two rocks.

"I figured that it would be in a chest with a big rusty lock on it," Cousin Jubal said, sniffing and crowding in to look at the treasure. "I wanted to bust the lock off."

Judge L. gently lifted the paper bag from its resting place and turned to face the excited boys. "Man, that's awfully deep to put such a small wad of treasure!" he said, his hands shaking uncontrollably in the anticipation of opening the paper container.

"It may be paper money, boys," Jake said, reaching for the paper bag gripped tightly in Judge L.'s dirty hand.

"Hold on there just a minute, Jake!" Judge L. shouted. "We just got the treasure dug up, and here you're already getting jumpy and greedy. Wait till it's your turn to look in this poke. We'll divide it up in four equal piles, so ever'body can have the same amount."

"Five piles," Tester corrected, crowding in with the rest to see what was in the paper bag.

"Four," Judge L. repeated. "You're not part of this expedition."

"I helped dig it up. Now I've got a share in it, too," Tester stated, preparing for a good argument for possession of the treasure—preparing for a fight if it should come to that.

"You'll have to knock me in the head first!" Judge L. stammered, anger showing in his shaky voice.

"We can arrange for that if it's necessary," Tester replied, warily edging closer to his friend.

Judge L. gripped the bag securely in his hand, protecting it against Tester's advances.

"You all forget about dividing the contents of that bag," Jake ordered. "Let's act like sensible grown-up adults. Look in there and see how much money's in it. That bag looks almost new to me. I can't believe that paper will last for a hundred years buried that deep in the damp ground."

Judge L. held the bag while the other boys crowded around him to see what was inside. "Back up, boys. Give me a little more scrouge," he said, trying to elbow the eager lads out of the way. After he had succeeded in moving the boys back to give him enough room to maneuver, he opened the bag. With unsteady, shaking hands he removed a carbide can. "It's awfully light," he said as he raised the can and shook it vigorously.

A faint swishing sound was all that emanated from the metal container.

Judge L. pried the lid from the top of the can with his barlow knife, reached inside, and withdrew a scrap of brown paper—part of another paper bag. He peered inside once more, and with disappointment showing in his trembling voice, he said to the eager, waiting boys, "Ain't nothing in there but a piece of paper." He threw the paper on the ground and put the lid back on the carbide can. Dejectedly, he threw the can as far down the mountainside as he could, then sat down on a rock.

"Wait a minute, boys!" Cousin Jubal shouted. "There's some writing of some sort on this scrap of poke-paper!" He picked it up and began to scan the words written on it—in green crayon.

Judge L. jumped up from his seat on the rock and crowded against Cousin Jubal, along with the other fellows. "What does it say? Is it a treasure map?" he asked excitedly, his spirits rising several notches.

"It says, 'I.O.U. one treasure. I hid this big pile of treasure many years ago. I got to needing some money to buy food and guns for my men, and my wife and kids needed some shoes and some clothes and some food. One of my little boys wanted a new bicycle, so I just had to dig it up. Sorry to disappoint you like this, but them's the fruits of treasure hunting. Better luck in the next hole you dig in. Yours truly, Rob L.'"

"I told you that it was probably a Confederate soldier that hid his fortunes," Judge L. said, reaching for the note. "Now, you'll believe things that I tell you about."

"He was real considerate to leave a note," Esker Seedy said. "At least he didn't dig it up without leaving a note 'splaining why he took it."

"Where would a Confederate soldier get a fortune?" Jake asked the excited boys. "The Confederates lost everything they had. They had to tie grapevines, ropes, and wire—anything they could get their hands on—around their shoes to hold them on. I think a man would have bought himself a pair of brogans if he had a fortune to bury. We've been made a fool of, and I know who did it to us."

"That's the general hisself!" Judge L. grinned. "Boy, I didn't think about him fighting big battles here on Coaley Creek! This place could go down in history as a great war memorial, a real shrine of some sort."

At the very bottom of the paper, in faint green letters, it read: "P.S.— over," with an arrow pointing to the edge of the paper.

Cousin Jubal flipped the paper over and began to read what was written on the other side. "'Boys, if you want a bicycle, you'll have to work for it.'"

"Let me see that note. That's just what I thought," Jake said, a big thistle-eating grin spreading over his face. "I know that Lee didn't have a green crayon to write a message with. Why should he leave a message? There was no treasure. That's Bart's scribbling. He's been here and dug in this good treasure hole and put that note in it just to plague us. I'd know his scribbling anywhere I saw it. Let's go home."

"Should we fill this hole up?" Judge L. asked, tossing a rock into the pit.

"Don't worry about it. I don't see any reason to fill it up," Jake replied. "Maybe another Confederate soldier will come by and fill it up when he hides another fortune. Let's go home, boys," he said, shaking his head, laughing at the prank that Bart had played on them.

"Yeah, let's go home, boys," Tester Seedy said, agreeing with Jake. "'Cause Mommy will whip me and you when we get over there," he sang.

Judge L. looked disappointed, but soon he was singing with the other boys, his voice blending in with the rest. He had dug a great treasure—a treasure of experience—from that hole in the ground. Treasures had to be earned, he realized. They weren't out there in holes, waiting patiently for someone to come along to dig them up. He ran to catch up with the departing lads.

"Mommy will whip me and you when we get over there," the boys sang as they descended the steep hill.

The Tater Chef

The years passed quickly. The Cornfield boys and girls grew up and began to scatter over the country. Beauty moved from Coaley Creek to the little town of Big Onion Gap, about ten miles from home. She stayed with an elderly couple and did domestic work for them. Dump volunteered for the U.S. Army and fought in North Africa during World War II, where he learned all about camping. He learned to pitch a tent, dig a foxhole, and pack camping equipment neatly so that it would not be too bulky when he tried to carry it over hill and dale without getting down in the back.

When Dump came home after the war—with an honorable discharge—he had sufficient leisure time to teach the youngsters all about camping. He wanted to go down on Bass Creek River and do a little fishing, and a lot of camping.

Usually when Dump had an urge to do something like that, the rest of the brothers, from Clem to Gillis, had the very same urge. The younger brothers looked up to Dump, since he was a United States Army veteran.

Clem, Jake, and Judge L. were working with their father for a coal company that was starting a new coal-mining operation across the big mountain from the Cornfields' house on Coaley Creek.

Jake and Judge L. were too young to be hired for regular employment, so Marn signed a paper which stated that he would accept all responsibilities for the two lads while they were on the job. Marn said that he could understand why the company did not want to hire the boys—they were too young to be carried on compensation insurance.

About the time Dump received his discharge, Bart was drafted into the Army. Bart went through basic training and shipped out overseas to Germany. The war had ended while he was still in basic training.

Marn and Vann were relieved when the wonderful news of the end of the war came over the battery radio that memorable morning.

"Do you boys have to work Saturday?" Dump asked Clem and Jake one afternoon.

"No, not this weekend," Clem replied. "We have to wait for a load of lumber and steel to come in before we can continue putting up the tipple. The supplies should be in early Monday morning, so that will give us a full weekend off to do what we want to."

"Will you be running coal through the tipple very soon?" Dump asked, continuing his questions about the operation's progress toward an early date for coal production.

"Not as soon as the company wants to, but I think they'll begin facing up the drift mouth pretty soon," Clem reported. "They're building roads and spreading base stone on them now, and hauling supplies in and stocking up for when they start digging coal."

"Are you going to work in the mines when you finish building the tipple?" Dump asked, pumping his brother for more information.

"No, I don't want anything to do with coal mining," Clem declared. "I ain't got anything against mining in general, but I want to work outside in the daylight. Me and Jake are planning to go to Baltimore, Maryland, to find us a job. We should have enough money to get up there on, after we finish the tipple. We've been saving almost all of our paychecks. We just spend the least we can get by with. We should have enough pretty soon. They say that you can find all kinds of jobs just lying around on the streets, waiting for someone from down here on Coaley Creek to come by and pick them up and start working them. Me and Jake are going to pick us up a couple of easy, good-paying jobs and start working as soon as we get there and get all settled in. Bertsie and Tarncie Brisco are going along with us to try to find them a couple of jobs."

"How are you boys going to get to Baltimore?" Dump asked. Before he received Clem's answer, he continued. "Those boys don't work anywhere. They ain't worked anywhere as far back as I can remember. They can't have any money, unless they have an income that nobody knows about. They're settin' you boys up, you know. They're going to let you pay their way up there. Then they'll sluve around and mooch off you just as long as you'll let them."

"Yeah, I know, but we'll make it fine," Clem came back. "They'll have to get a job or starve, as far as I care."

"Are you boys going to take the bus?" Dump wanted to know.

"Tarncie and Bertsie have an old A-Model Ford—runs good—and he says that all of us can ride in it if it don't rain, and if we don't take a big grip of clothes and things," Jake said.

"Do you think you can make it in that old trap? I've not seen it, but any car those two can afford has to be a trap. I bet it's held together with bale-hay wire," Dump laughed.

"Tarncie says that the name on the front of his car is all that he needs, plus a little gas," Jake replied.

"Plus a *lot* of gas, to get you all the way to Baltimore," Dump said. "Man, that's over five hundred miles from Coaley Creek! But there's nothing like confidence when anyone's traveling in an old car like that."

"We'll make it," Clem vowed.

"The mines pay good money, and they're right here at the back door, so to speak. You boys can get jobs right at home. You don't have to go to Baltimore," Dump stated.

"What about you, Dump?" Clem asked. "What are you going to do since you got your honorable discharge from the Army? Are you going to work in the mines?"

"No, I'm going to study electricity and radio repairs," Dump replied. "Television's going to be a hot item one of these days now. Television will probably be bigger than radio before you know it. I might study television repairs, too."

"There ain't any radio and television schools around here," Clem said.

"I'm going to Chicago, to a big school there," Dump told him.

"How can you do that?" Clem wanted to know. "You don't have any money to go away to school on."

"I'll go on the GI Bill that was passed for veterans to get an education or vocational training of some kind," Dump replied, answering Clem. "I'll have to take the vocational training, since I didn't graduate from high school."

"The mines are right at your back door, as you said. Take advantage of that," Clem said.

"I don't want to start in the mines," Dump replied. "What are you going to do in Baltimore, Jake?" he asked, changing the subject.

"I'll look for a mechanic's job in a big garage or filling station," Jake answered. "I'm interested in repairing cars. I'll pick my guitar and sing with a country band in one of the big night clubs. I hear that the night clubs pay big money for part-time pickers. Before you know it, with my mechanic's job and the extra pay for picking my guitar and singing good ballads, I'll have a pot full of money. If I don't go to Baltimore and get me a job, me and Cousin Brownlo might join up with the Navy. I'll take up some kind of vocational training—welding probably. I've learned a lot on the job while working with Arlis Pervis. He's a number one welder."

"I'm not going to join any branch of service," Judge L. said, entering the room. "I can make a lot more money by working over on Lick Fork for that construction company than I can in the Army."

Judge L. held a contrivance which he called a pistol. Where he got the modified gun, no one knew, for none of the brothers had seen it before.

"Where did you get that gizmo?" Dump asked, noticing the altered gun. "Here, let me see that thing." He took it, looked it over, shook his head slowly from side to side, then handed the gun back to Judge L.

"I found it rolling up a hill in a cow's track," Judge L. replied, and that was all that he would say.

"I've heard that before," Dump laughed. "Now, where did you get it?"

"I found it rolling up a hill in a cow's track," Judge L. repeated.

"Has Dad seen that thing?" Dump asked.

"Yeah, he's seen it. He knows about it," Judge L. replied. "You fellers are getting real inquisitive all of a sudden."

"Where did you tell Dad you got it?" Clem queried, and got the same answer that Dump had received.

"Rolling up a hill in a cow's track in the rain," Judge L. said, grinning all over the room.

"I hope Dad didn't take exception to it," Dump laughed, wondering what his father had said about Judge L.'s gun.

"Well, Brother, he wasn't very impressed with it, but he didn't cut a big shine about it," Judge L. began. "Actually, he did say that it was worth something; not in them exact words. He told me to tape a nickel to it and throw it away. He said that I could tell people that I threw something away then."

"Dad had a good point there," Dump laughed.

Judge L. had traded for an altered rifle—a twenty-two caliber. Someone had cut the barrel off, along with the stock. It was a bolt-action, single-shot rifle. There would have been little doubt of the outcome had he met up with one of those gunslingers from a western movie. He could not fan the hammer with one of his hands, but Judge L. had no plans to meet up with any bad guys.

"You can take that one-shot, bolt-action pistol camping with us Friday evening," Dump informed Judge L.

"Camping!" Judge L. shouted with excitement, swinging the altered gun over his head.

"Camping!" Teed shouted. Until then he had listening quietly, and that was unusual for Teed, since he was so hyperactive. "I'm ready to go camping right now, if the rest wants to. I stay ready, and I'll be raring to go Friday night."

"I don't know about that," Dump said, rubbing Teed's cotton-white head. "I'll have to ask Dad and Mom before I take you and Gillis along. It's still pretty cold at night this time of year."

"Don't you worry yourself about me and Gillis," Teed said. "We're a couple of tough little nuts."

"I don't know about the tough part, but I do know that you're nuts," Judge L. quipped.

Teed and Gillis didn't think Judge L. was very funny, but the other boys thought he was, laughing their approval of the wisecrack.

"I'll go hunt Dad up and ask him right now," Teed said, rising and running through the house in search of his father. He found Marn on the front porch, resting after a hard day's work.

"Can I go down on Bass Creek River camping and fishing with Dump and the rest of the boys and Gillis, too?" Teed asked. He jumped up and down excitedly, impatiently awaiting an answer.

"It's too cold for little fellers like you and Gillis to go traipsing off to Bass Creek River on a camping trip," Marn told Teed.

"We won't be traipsing off to Bass Creek River. We're going camping down there, and fishing, too," Teed replied. "Dump and the others are going Friday."

"We'll have to wait until Friday and see," Marn said. "We don't know what the weather will be like on that day. It could be too cold for you and Gillis to camp out this early in the spring."

Teed ran back to report to Dump on his father's answer. "He said that I could go," he beamed, smiling all over himself.

"Are you sure he said you could go?" Dump asked, attempting to get a truthful answer from Teed.

"He said to wait and see about the weather on Friday," Teed said. "That's just about the same as saying that I can go."

"You can watch the thermometer," Dump told him. "If the temperature's warm on Friday, you can go, but if it's not, you'll have to stay at home. Is that fair?"

"No, 'cause I want to go camping," Teed whined. "Just 'cause I'm little don't mean that I'm not real tough and able to do what you big boys can."

"Let's wait until Friday. We can talk more about it then," Dump suggested, rising from his seat on the back porch. He rubbed Teed's head. "Don't worry about it. Things could look a lot better by Friday. It could turn off real warm. You know that the weather is very changeable in May. We may not even have to wear our shirts," he explained, trying to encourage the lad.

*   *   *   *

Friday dawned rainy and cold for May. Sheets of rain splashed against the windows as the wind carried the water along in its wake. The temperature had dropped drastically—to forty-two degrees Fahrenheit.

Teed and Gillis kept an eye on the thermometer to see if they could detect a change in the temperature.

It was still raining when Marn, Clem, Jake, and Judge L. came home from work early, and it continued to rain throughout the afternoon.

"It went up one temperature," Gillis shouted, running through the house in search of Dump. He found Dump in the front room, talking with Marn and trying to keep the fire warm.

"It went up one degree," Dump corrected, attempting to explain the principles of a thermometer to Gillis. "Temperature is measured in degrees. If the red line goes up or down, the movement is in degrees, not in temperatures."

"Well, I see what you mean," Gillis beamed, his brown eyes sparkling. "It moves in degrees, not temperatures like you said, Teed."

"Well, I told you something. I didn't leave you in the dark on the matter," Teed claimed.

"Fellers," Marn said, addressing the boys, "let Dump and the big boys go camping this time. Maybe you can go next time if the weather's warm."

"Why can't we go this time?" the little fellows whined in response to their father's suggestion.

"Now don't yammer about it. If you whimper about it like babies, then you can't go the next time, either," Marn warned.

"All right," Teed grumbled, showing disappointment with the stern verdict. He knew not to argue. Arguing would only get him a good stropping. Marn wouldn't put up with back talk.

Gillis could not restrain his emotions. He began to cry openly as he followed Teed into another room where they could pout.

*　*　*　*

Late that afternoon, Dump, Clem, Jake, and Judge L. left on their trip to Bass Creek River. They looked forward to a long weekend of recreation. If the rain should stop, the fellows would camp in the open, but if it continued as it had all day, they would have to pitch camp—without tents—under a huge cliff near the edge of the river.

Seldom Seedy, Bertsie Brisco, Tarncie Brisco, and Cousin Brownlo Cornfield met Dump and his brothers where Coaley Creek and Big Bull Creek merged to form the winding Bass Creek River.

Each of the fellows carried a homemade knapsack filled with food, fishing gear, cooking utensils, and blankets for their bedding.

"We have enough food and equipment for a full regiment," Dump said as they walked along the rough path that ran in a snake-like trace parallel to the river. "We'll make camping a regular weekend event. Nothing will change our plans, and I mean nothing at all. How does that sound to ever'-body? Do you agree on that?"

"Agreed!" came the happy reply.

"I don't want to get caught cold and hungry," Seldom Seedy said, shifting the weight of his pack from one shoulder to the other.

"Me, neither," Cousin Brownlo spoke up, trying to keep pace with the others, "so I brought lots of blankets and taters."

"Is that all the food that you brought?" Tarncie Brisco asked. "That's what I brought, too."

"Yeah, 'cause I figured that some of the rest would bring bread, grease, salt, and stuff like that," Cousin Brownlo replied, looking around at the blank faces gawking back at him in disbelief.

"We brought taters, too," Seldom Seedy said, speaking for Bertsie Brisco and himself.

"I brought taters, too," Clem Cornfield intoned, looking at the others in surprise.

"Our diet won't vary from day to day," Dump said, laughing at the efforts of communication used while organizing the camping trip. "Jake, I suppose you brought taters, too."

"No, I didn't," Jake declared. "I brought a can of chopped meat and a box of crackers. And I also brought a dab of cheese, plus some mayonnaise. Yeah, and I brought a big onion. It smells strong enough to kill a horse."

"Boy, you sure have a feast compared to our meager fare," Seldom Seedy moaned.

"We can have one good meal of mixed foods, then a million meals of taters," Dump laughed. "I'll do some of the cooking. I learned how to fix taters a lot of different ways in the Army."

"If you can cook Army taters, then you must have been a cook 'stead of a soldier in the Army," Tarncie Brisco said.

"I was no cook, but I learned how the cook made the different types of taters," Dump professed.

"Boys, Dump can be our tater chef," Clem joked, laughing hilariously.

"I guess I will," Dump agreed, laughing with Clem.

"What was the Army like, Dump?" Tarncie wanted to know.

"It had its good points, and its bad points, but I guess the good outweighed the bad," Dump said. A row of thought wrinkles furrowed his forehead. "The battles are best forgotten, if possible. But the days of basic training and the trip overseas hold some fond moments of memory."

"Tell us how you learned about camping and packing gear for your marches," Tarncie suggested.

"Memory of the marches is best forgotten," Dump mumbled, drawn once more into deep thought. He commenced to tell the younger fellows about some of his military experiences, holding them spellbound by his great stories until they arrived at their proposed campsite just as darkness began to settle over the river and surrounding hills.

There were several miles of woods along the crooked river, with no houses or signs of human habitation near the remote campsite—the main reason for selecting that particular place to camp.

A light rain continued to fall, but there wasn't enough moisture to dampen the campers' spirits, nor the campsite beneath a large cliff hovering over the edge of the river. A powdery, slate-gray dust covered the camping area.

A smoke-blackened wall indicated that other adventurers had frequented the place. There were boys' and girls' initials in crudely drawn hearts on the rock wall. Empty cans, bread and cake wrappers, and the bones of a variety of animals cluttered the unkempt cliff floor.

"The people that camped here last sure was bad housekeepers," Cousin Brownlo Cornfield said, pointing to the trash.

"They sure were," Judge L. agreed.

"Let's police the place," Dump recommended, using some of his military jargon.

"Yeah, we'll lock up everybody in jail that threw down all this trash," Judge L. verified, slinking about in a crouched position, imitating a person in search of something elusive.

"'Policing' the area means to check it out and clean it up," Dump returned, laughing at Judge L.

"Oh, that'll be easy," Judge L. remarked, rising to a normal position. He ran to pick up a bread wrapper that was partially covered by leaves and dirt.

"Fellers," Dump said as he began to instruct the boys on how to organize their work detail, "put all bits of paper and bones in one pile, and the cans, bottles, and pieces of broken glass in another pile. When we build our campfire, we can use the paper as kindling, and after the fire gets hot enough, the bones will burn up."

"What can we do with the pile of cans and glass?" Bertsie asked, throwing a piece of broken pop bottle on top of a growing pile of debris near the wall of the cliff.

"We can leave them in a pile until tomorrow. Then we can dig a hole and bury them," Dump said, explaining the procedure to follow in disposing of the unwanted rubbish.

"How about throwing the stuff in the river?" Cousin Brownlo proposed. "That'd get rid of it in a hurry."

"That'd pollute the river, and there should be a law against throwing trash and junk into the country's rivers and streams," Dump stated.

"That stuff won't hurt the water any worse than letting raw sewage run into the river," Clem said. "You know how the towns allow the stuff from bathroom toilets to run into it. A little wad of cans won't hurt the water any worse than that guck running into it."

"You have a point there, Clem, but our doing something wrong just because others do doesn't mean that we are right if we do the same thing," Dump said.

The boys worked feverishly in their efforts to clean up the camping area so they could build a fire.

Dump found a small pile of dry firewood against the wall of the cliff. "This will be about enough to get a fire going, but we'll have to gather more to keep it burning all night," he said. He succeeded in his efforts to light a fire. The flames gave off a soft, beautiful light that made grotesque shadows dance eerily all about the campsite.

Clem lit a carbide lamp and set it on a rock at a level which let the light flood the entire cliff floor and the surrounding woods.

"Get some more firewood, boys, while I cook up a tater feast," Dump said, peeling potatoes and dropping them into a bucket filled with water from a clear stream that ran from the cliff wall. "Can we fry your can of chopped meat, Jake?" he asked as he finished peeling the potatoes. He began to slice the potatoes and place the pieces in a black skillet on the open fire. "We'll have plenty fish to fry tomorrow to go with our endless supply of taters. We might have good luck with some night fishing. Let's eat good tonight. We'll not worry about tomorrow till it gets here."

"Sure, go ahead and cook it," Jake replied, taking the can of meat from his knapsack and tossing it to Dump.

"I'm going to run a trotline across the river just below the ripples there in the bend," Cousin Brownlo announced, pointing toward the muddy torrent. "We'll have a good mess of fish when we check it in the morning. Let's get a supply of firewood and then go set that trotline."

Even though they could not see the river, everyone looked in the direction Cousin Brownlo had pointed.

Everyone, except Dump, went into the wet forest in search of dead wood for the campfire. Clem led the way, his carbide light penetrating the wall of darkness.

The boys returned after about fifteen minutes and placed their loads of wood in a neat pile against the cliff wall.

Dump served up a meal of charred potatoes and crunchy meat.

Brownlo, Tarncie, Bertsie, and Seldom forgot to bring forks, plates, and drinking cups. They had to wait while the rest ate, to use the same utensils.

Seldom Seedy was famished and began to eat from the skillets, using his dirty fingers. The other three hungry boys joined him in a mad assault on the food. They were like a bunch of slopping-hogs, slurping and gnyamming the burnt grub.

"Don't you boys have any table manners at all?" Dump asked, showing disgust as he watched the crude manner in which the boys disposed of the food.

"Yeah, we have manners, but we left them at home with our plates and things," Seldom said, gobbling down a piece of crisp meat and a handful of fried potatoes.

"We don't need manners out here in the woods," Cousin Brownlo mumbled through a full mouth, sopping up the last of the burnt scraps of potatoes the tater chef had cooked. He looked around hungrily. Finding nothing else to gobble up, he sighed contentedly and lay down on a blanket to rest for a spell.

Supper was over, the cooking utensils washed and stored for the night, and all scraps of garbage were placed on the fire to burn.

Seldom, Tarncie, Bertsie, Cousin Brownlo, and Clem had gone to the river to string a trotline across it—below the riffles.

Judge L. lay on his back with his feet toward the warm fire. With a full stomach of fried potatoes and chopped meat, he had drifted off to sleep.

Jake smiled wickedly as he took a burning chunk of wood from the fire, placed it against the sole of one of his brother's rubber boots, and then lay back down at a safe distance to wait for the boot to get hot and wake Judge L. from his peaceful slumber. He did not have long to wait.

Judge L. screamed in agony, bounded to his feet, and began to hop about in an effort to remove the smoldering boot from his hot foot. "Jake, you crazy thing!" he yelled, trying unsuccessfully to rid his foot of the boot.

Jake was brought to a ready-to-flee alertness as Judge L. continued to scream and hop about on one foot, stirring up the dust.

Judge L. finally succeeded in removing his hot boot. "You've had it, Jake," he threatened. Holding the smoldering shoe at the ready, he advanced toward his brother.

"I'll see you later on in the season," Jake said as he exited the area, running for the protection of the dark woods.

A piercing scream of agony shattered the night as Jake fell and tumbled down the embankment at the edge of the cliff.

"I hope you broke your neck!" Judge L. grumbled, returning to his blanket near the fire. He picked up one of Jake's shoes from its resting place near the fire, where Jake had put them to dry, and threw it into the flames, then sat down to rub his blistered foot.

"Dump, come quick! I'm hurt real bad!" Jake screamed. "I stepped on that meat can that we emptied for our supper. I threw it into the bushes instead of putting it on the trash heap."

Dump and Judge L. hurried to Jake and carried him to the fire. They made him as comfortable as they could and began to make a thorough examination of the injured foot.

Blood gushed from a nasty-looking cut on the bottom of Jake's right foot—just behind the big toe.

Using some of his military training in first aid, Dump placed his handkerchief directly to the bleeding wound and applied pressure. He gripped Jake's leg with his other hand to try to help stem the free-flowing blood. "Go get Clem and the others, Judge L. The river's making too much noise for you to get their attention by hollering, so run as fast as you can and tell them to come in a hurry. We'll have to get Jake fixed up the best we can and carry him out of here to a doctor. That cut's too bad to take the chance of staying here till tomorrow. He'll need a tetanus shot to prevent lockjaw. I think I have the bleeding slowed down and under control, but hurry." He removed his shirt, tore a strip from it, and bandaged the lacerated foot.

Judge L. stumbled around with his rubber boot, trying to put it back on his foot.

The charred remains of Jake's shoe lay among the hot embers. He wouldn't need the shoe, since he couldn't put it on his injured foot.

Judge L. finally succeeded in his effort to get his blistered foot into the boot, and, taking a weak flashlight, he ran into the dark night, returning shortly with the other boys following close behind.

"What happened?" Clem asked, gasping for breath. He took a good look at the blood-stained bandage and winced.

"Jake stepped on an empty meat can and cut his foot almost off," Dump replied. "Cut two long poles and tie a blanket over them to make a stretcher. We've got to get him to a doctor as soon as possible. He needs some stitches to close up that cut. It's going to be a long, hard trip, but we have to do it. We can't stay here all night."

"Cousin Lemon Eskers lives up the holler from where we turned down Bass Creek River," Seldom Seedy informed Dump. "We can take him there. Him and his wife, Dusty, can tend to that cut tonight, and then tomorrow you can get somebody to take him to the doctor. I don't think you can do any better than that tonight. Actually, that's about the only choice you have."

"I guess you're right," Dump agreed. "Come on boys. Let's get started."

"There goes my chance to go to Baltimore with you boys," Jake wailed, grimacing with pain as he gripped his foot with both hands. "I won't be able to help finish building that tipple with the construction company, either. I've really messed up your plans, boys."

"We'll wait for you to get better," Clem said, trying to encourage the injured boy.

"I should have watched where I was running," Jake whined.

"You should have put that meat can in the pile of rubbish 'stead of throwing it out into the bushes," Dump reminded him. "Let's get him out of here, fellers. Standing here talking about it won't get him to a doctor."

Dump, Clem, Tarncie, and Cousin Brownlo gently raised the stretcher and started toward Lemon Eskers' house.

"See that the fire is extinguished before you leave," Dump called over his shoulder. He heard a sizzling sound as Judge L. doused the fire with a bucket of water.

"We'll have to retrieve that trotline," Seldom said. "Let me borrow your carbide light, Clem. It won't take me more than a jiffy to get down to the river and pull it up. I can save it for our next trip down here. Line and hooks cost good money, you know."

"You can just forget that trotline, fellers," Dump said, trying to hurry everyone along in order to get the injured boy to Lemon Eskers' house for some much-needed medical attention. "You can run back down here in the morning and get it if you're so set in taking it up.

*   *   *   *

When the tiring trip and the long night of waiting and worrying finally ended, Dump started the ten-mile trip to Big Onion Gap to get a doctor. When he couldn't find anyone there to go to Bass Creek River to get Jake and take him to the doctor, he asked the doctor to go to Jake.

With several sutures and a thick bandage, Jake was pronounced able to go home.

The trotline across the riffles in the bend of the river was forgotten, and there were no more camping trips to Bass Creek River for many weeks while Jake recuperated from the injury to his foot.

Short Shot

Esker Seedy was boasting to Teed Cornfield and his other buddies about what he would be receiving as his Christmas present. "I'll be getting a new bicycle. My old one is a year old now. The thing's about shot and ready for the trash heap."

"That's 'cause you're too rough on it," Satch Hood commented. "You never clean it up and oil it."

"I'll take your old bicycle if it's ready for the trash heap," Teed offered excitedly, thinking that he might get a bicycle—the one thing that he had hoped would be his present every Christmas morning as far back as he could remember. "I'm pretty gifted at mechanical fixing. I can have that pile of junk running in no time at all."

"No, you won't get that bicycle!" Tester Seedy retorted. "I get all the hand-me-downs at our house. Esker's bicycle ain't much of a hand-me-down, but it'll be mine after Christmas. So, it's hands off to you Teed."

"Ain't you gonna get a new bike, too, Tester?" Gillis asked. "Santy can bring both of you a brand-new bike at the same time. He can bring two as easy as one, and he's got a store chock-full of nothing in it but new bicycles."

"How do you know that he's got a store full of just bicycles?" Satch Hood asked.

"'Cause he's got plenty of everything that you can possibly think of, so he could have a whole store full of bicycles," Gillis said defiantly.

"You're just guesstimating about how many bikes that Santy's got. Gillis, you're bad to reckon about things without really knowing what you're talking about," Satch remarked.

"I know as much as you do about Christmas and Santy!" Gillis stormed. "So Santy could bring two bikes to the same house. There ain't anything wrong with my saying that he has a store full of bicycles. I know he has. He's got everything you can think of."

"We'll just get one bike at our house this year. The chimbley is too little for Santy to get two bikes down it at the same time," Esker said, ignoring Gillis. "That's why I'm the only one that's gonna get a new bike this year. Tester will have to wait till I get too big to ride a bike before he can get one of his own."

"You don't get too big to ride a bicycle," Gillis said. "And Santy can bring one bicycle down the chimbley, and then go back and get another one. Santy's smart enough to think of doing it that way 'stead of trying to struggle with two at once. You boys try to make Santy out to be a big dummy that don't know anything."

"Santy ain't a dummy, and he can bring two bikes, but we're just gonna get one bike so that Santy won't have to work so hard," Esker explained. "You said that people don't get too big to ride a bike, Gillis. I know that a person don't get too big to ride a bike, but you get so old that you don't want to ride one. Dad don't want to ride a bicycle anymore."

"Yeah, but Talmage is probably Dan'l Boone's uncle, so that would certainly make him too old to ride a bicycle. That's too old to even think about riding a bicycle," Teed said, trying to take some of the pressure off Gillis in the dispute about the age to stop riding a bicycle.

"Another reason for Santy's bringing just one bicycle to our house is that he don't have time to make two trips down the chimbley as he delivers presents on Christmas night," Esker told his friends. "He's pressed for time, and he has to shake a leg to get all his rounds made before daylight. He has such a long trip to make, and I just don't see how he can make it in one night. He'd have to have a lot of help to get around to ever'body in the world and on Coaley Creek. I'm beginning to wonder about this Santy thing. I'm beginning to wonder if there's really a Santy Claus doing all this bringing at Christmas. I'll tell you what I think about it. I believe that it might be our daddies and mommies doing this present bringing."

"It can't be our dad and mom bringing the presents at our house," Gillis said. "They don't have enough extra money to buy presents with."

"It don't matter to me where they come from, just so's I get 'em," Satch

Hood said. "I allus get plenty presents. I don't worry about who has to pay for them."

"Why is it that Santy brings you and Esker and Tester a lot of different presents, and he brings Teed and me just one little bitty present?" Gillis wondered.

"I can't answer that," Satch Hood said, scratching his head in thought.

"I can answer you," Esker volunteered, laughing. "It's 'cause me and Tester and Satch are much better boys than you and Teed."

"I know better than that, Esker," was Teed's quick reply. "But I don't understand why Santy shows favoritism in a bunch of kids from the same holler. I thought that he was ever'body's Santy Claus. You boys allus get lots of toys and everything, but I've never got what I asked for. I've even set on Santy's boney knee and asked him personal to bring me a big list of things for Christmas, but he's never brought me anything that I asked for. Now tell me that he don't show favoritism." Teed was hot about the thought that Santa Claus could like some kids better than others, even if they lived in the same community. Maybe Esker was right, maybe his parents bought the Christmas presents and put them in his cap each year.

"I'm beginning to think the same thing," Gillis agreed. "I think Santy is prejudiced. He brings ever'body else bicycles, wagons, cap busters, and lots of other good toys, but me and Teed don't hardly get anything."

"You boys are going to have to get on the good side of Santy, and then you'll get things like me and Esker," Tester said, grinning and strutting around with his thumbs behind his galluses. "We're special folks to Santy."

"You ain't no specialer than me and Teed!" Gillis stormed back.

"Do you get big presents like me and Esker and Satch do?" Tester asked, still grinning and taunting Gillis.

"No, but that ain't fair," Gillis whined.

"I guess it's 'cause you all have too many kids in your family," Satch said, trying to help Teed and Gillis in their argument with the Seedys.

"I guess you're right there, Satch," Teed allowed. "But it looks to me like he could give you boys less and divvy up some more to our big family. Just 'cause we're a big family don't mean that we should be slighted and get less than others that don't have as many children."

"Why don't you tell him about it—Santy that is?" Esker suggested.

"I can't get to see him now. I can't get to Big Onion Gap to that big store where he hangs out at all the time. And it's only two days till he makes his rounds on Coaley Creek." Teed grumbled.

The five boys walked along the rocky road, making their way home from school that Friday afternoon. Their Christmas holiday had begun with the dismissal of classes at the end of the school day, with two long weeks with nothing to do but play with new Christmas toys.

The boys talked about many different things as they walked along the rough road, but Christmas was the most interesting subject of all.

Teed kicked an empty cream can as he walked along. He had found the can beside the road. Most likely, a dog had abandoned it there after having learned that it could not get to the cankered remains of the evaporated milk that had dried up and stuck to the bottom.

Occasionally there was a scramble for the can as all five boys made a mad dash for it at the same time.

Esker Seedy managed to get his big foot ahead of the others on the last wild scamper. The can banged over the rocks in the road as Esker slammed it a good lick with his big brogan. When the can came to a stop, there was another mad rush to kick it again.

The competition continued for a while, but soon Teed was the lone kicker, the rest tiring of the game.

"What did you get for Christmas last year, Teed?" Satch asked, breaking a period of silence in which the only sound had been the shuffling of the boys' feet and the banging of the can bouncing over the rocks after Teed gave it a kick.

"I got some fruits and candy and nuts in my cap," he replied, continuing to play the can-kicking game.

"In your cap? Why in your cap?" Satch asked, looking at Teed with surprise smeared all over his face.

"We allus put down our caps with our names in them so that Santy will know whose cap it is and what to leave for each of us," Teed replied.

"That's why you don't get a bicycle, Gillis. Santy can't get a bicycle in a cap," Tester laughed.

"He could bring me a bicycle and hang my cap on the handlebars for me," Gillis quipped.

"What do you put down for Santy to put your things in, Tester?" Teed asked, running to kick the can again.

"I hang up one of my socks," Tester told him. "I hang up a stocking like in olden days. I carry on the old-timey tradition. Maybe that's why you don't get much. You're breaking the tradition."

"I ain't breaking a tradition, and I know for a fact that Santy can't get a bicycle in a sock, unless it's a giant's sock," Teed laughed. "There's something fishy about you getting ever'thing that you say you get, when all you have is just a sock to put it in. Gosh! I wouldn't eat any candy that Santy put in your stinking stocking!"

"It's a clean sock that I hang up, mind you," Tester replied, showing exasperation toward Teed.

"What did you get—other than candy, nuts, and stuff like that—Teed?" Esker asked. "What kind of toys did you get? Or did you even get a toy?"

"Yeah, I got a toy—a little rubber truck," Teed said. "And do you know what? The price was still on it. It cost Santy ten cents."

"Boy, that sure was cheap! If Santy had took the price tag off, you wouldn't have got anything at all," Esker said, laughing at his own joke, but the others did not laugh with him.

"I know that it would have been almost less than nothing with the price gone," Teed said, agreeing with his friend. "I still say that Santy likes you boys a lot better than me and Gillis."

After a lull in the exciting conversation, Satch Hood spoke. "Teed, why don't you stay up on Christmas night and confront Santy and tell him to divvy up more toys at your house? Just tell him that there are a lot more people living in that house than he thinks. Maybe he'll leave a few extra things to make his toy sack lighter. You'll just have to speak up if you want more toys. If you don't ask, you won't get anything extra is all I can tell you."

"We can't stay up on Christmas night," Gillis said. "Dad and Mom say that Santy will throw ashes in our eyes as he comes down the chimbley if we're standing there gawking at him. Santy ain't supposed to be seen when he brings presents. No, Satch, we'll have to pass on that suggestion. I don't want ashes in my eyes. I'll have to take what he leaves for me and make the best of it."

"Well, that's your loss, not mine," Satch told him.

Esker and Tester Seedy left the other boys when they arrived at their house beside the road. The conversation about Christmas ended with their departure.

Satch, Teed, and Gillis walked on toward the head of Coaley Creek, with Teed still kicking the cream can, even though it was bent and mangled. It was so badly bent that it would have been impossible to recognize it as a cream can.

Teed and Gillis wondered why they weren't at the top of Santa's list like the Seedys and Satch Hood. It was a mystery to them. They knew that their friends weren't lying about their gifts. They had witnessed the presence of the presents at their homes while visiting on different occasions. They couldn't understand why there was partiality shown amongst the boys who lived on Coaley Creek.

"I guess it's not meant to be understood by children our ages, Gillis," Teed told his little brother. "But we sure had a lot of fun with our little rubber trucks that Santy brought us last year. We hauled a lot of dirt in them before they wore plum' out."

"Yeah, and if that dirt had been gold, we would be zillionaires today," Gillis reflected.

That little joke made them laugh. Their conversation turned to matters of lesser interest.

*   *   *   *

"Dad," Gillis said that Christmas Eve, after supper was over and the dishes were cleared from the long table, "me and Teed are going to sit up till

Santy comes tonight."

"You boys had better get to bed early so Santy can come early," Marn replied, amused with Gillis' idea of waiting up for Santa's arrival. "And," he told them, "Santy has lots of other kids to visit tonight—all over the world. Surely you don't want to keep him on Coaley Creek all night and let other little kids do without Christmas presents. You know that he don't have much time to dally around. He has to go to other children's houses, too. He can tell when somebody's up at a house just as he lands on the roof. If he sees that somebody is still up waiting for him, he'll just bypass that house and go on to the next one. So you'd better get to bed early."

"We'll sit real still right in front of the fireplace, and then when we hear Santy, we'll pl'ike we're asleep," Gillis said. "Then, if he comes in and gives us a bunch of good toys, he can go on if he wants to. If it's too late for him to go all over the world, he can stay and play awhile with us."

"I'm going to wait up and see him and ask him why he don't bring me and Gillis what we ask for each year," Teed informed his smiling father.

"Maybe other kids need things a lot more than you do is why you don't always get ever'thing you want," their mother said in an effort to assure her sons that Santa would leave toys for them if any were left after he had first given toys to the needy.

"If anyone is worse off than we are, I'd hate to spend a Christmas with him," Gillis said. "Mom, you said that maybe because others need more than me and Teed is why we don't always get what we want. You should say that we always *don't* get what we want. This Christmas, though, I'm gonna make sure I get ever'thing that I want, and then some. Me and Teed's gonna sit smack-dab in front of the fireplace. When Santy sticks his head out of the chimbley, we're gonna throw ashes in *his* eyes so *he* can't see. Then we're gonna go out to his sled and pick out our own toys. He'd better have plenty of things left in his storehouse, 'cause we're gonna clean out that sleigh. We'll toss all dolls and girl presents. We won't need any girl things. Santy will have to go back to his storehouse and fill his sled up again. We're gonna stay up, ain't we, Teed?"

"You're right about that, Gillis," Teed replied. "The Cornfields' house is gonna be crammed full of good toys this Christmas. Santy will know what we want for next year—that will be everything that he can haul in his sled."

"It'll be a long wait," Marn smiled, seeing the determination in the two little boys. "It's going to get cold tonight—might snow. When the fire goes out, you boys will freeze your noses."

"We can take any cold that comes along, can't we, Gillis?" Teed stated.

"Yeah, I can stand anything for toys," Gillis replied, his big brown eyes reflecting the light from the fire.

"You'll have to let the fire go out so that Santy can come down the chimney," Vann told them.

"That's all right," Gillis said. "We'll let it cool off so Santy can bring us some Christmas presents."

"Put your caps where Santy can find them," their mother ordered. "Then get to bed."

"We're staying up to see Santy," Gillis replied. "The rest of you can go to bed anytime you get ready."

"Let's go to bed, Mom. Let these boys stay up if they want to," Marn chuckled, rising from his seat before the warm fireplace. "They'll probably freeze out before too long."

When the parents retired for the night, Teed and Gillis put two straight-back chairs close to the fire. They began their vigil, waiting for the arrival of jolly ol' Santa Claus. They wanted to make their own selections from his sleigh. He wouldn't be so jolly after Gillis popped him in the eyes with ashes.

Teed and Gillis whispered for a while, discussing their strategy, waiting for Santa's arrival. They hoped that he wouldn't be late.

Gillis raked a handful of ashes from beneath the fireplace grate and let them cool off enough to be able to grip them in his hand while he waited for Santa to come.

Thirty minutes passed, approached an hour, and then two hours. As the fire burned down to only winking embers, the ashes slowly fell from a relaxed little hand. Gillis slumped over against Teed—asleep—and soon Teed lay his head against Gillis—asleep.

"Boys, you'd better wake up. Santy came and left some stuff," Vann called to Teed and Gillis early that Christmas morning.

"How did we get in this bed, Gillis?" Teed wanted to know.

"Beats the tar out of me," Gillis came back. "The last thing I can remember was sitting in front of the fireplace waiting for Santy to come."

"Well, I guess Santy put you in the bed," Vann said, shaking Skatney and Friday to wake them up.

The sisters jumped out of their bed on the opposite side of the room.

"Look what Santy left us!" Skatney shouted as she entered the front bedroom, where the caps lay on the treadle-type Singer sewing machine. Each cap was filled to the brim with goodies.

Skatney's excited cry brought Teed and Gillis out of their warm feather bed. As they entered the other bedroom, they were greeted by Skatney, Friday, and a crackling fire.

Skatney stood before the warm fire, a banana in one hand and a stick of hard candy in her other hand. She alternated her hands to her mouth, first one hand, then the other. She took bites from each, mixing the flavors. Skatney didn't care for toys. She liked to eat.

"What did you get, Skatney?" Teed asked his sister.

Skatney mumbled something that Teed did not understand due to a mouthful of banana and candy, which she chewed loudly, relishing the good flavor of her Christmas goodies.

"Where's my bicycle?" Gillis asked, frantically running around the room.

Teed was just as distraught as Gillis as he followed his little brother's every step.

"Santy couldn't get as big a thing as a bicycle down the chimney," his mother replied, attempting to soothe Gillis' disappointment.

"Where's my bicycle?" Gillis continued to ask, running helter-skelter about the room. "Esker Seedy and Satch Hood get big presents down their chimbleys," he whined. "Why couldn't Santy get one down ours? Our chimbley is just as big as theirs is."

"It's because you boys stayed up too late last night," Vann told him. "Next year you'll have to get to bed on time."

"Santy's like Miss Wills, our teacher," Gillis moaned. "Miss Wills' got pets in school. Josie Milt's her pet. Esker, Tester, and Satch are Santy's pets. He brings them bicycles and big things to prove it." He continued to whine and show his distress.

"Maybe he didn't bring them bicycles, either, this year," Skatney commented between mouthfuls of goodies, trying to raise Gillis' spirits. She did not worry about gifts, while the good food lasted, that is.

"Yeah, he could've done just that," Jake agreed, entering the room. "I found four presents under my bed. I wonder where they came from. I found two girls' gifts and two boys' gifts. Hey, they've got names on them!" He gripped the gifts in his arms. "Skatney," he said, handing his sister a package. "Friday." He placed a bulky parcel in the little outstretched hands waiting for a present.

Teed's and Gillis' gifts were similar in size and shape, with an identical lump on the side of each.

Skatney and Friday received dolls. They walked about the room playing with them, holding them close to their breasts, singing lullabies to them.

Gillis tore the pretty-colored paper from the neatly wrapped gift. His eyes bugged out as he stared open-mouthed at the black toy pistol with white handles.

With shaking hands Teed opened his gift. In his excitement he dropped his beautiful gun—identical to the one that Gillis held in his hand. It slipped from the imitation-leather holster and landed on the hard floor. The sudden impact broke the exquisite toy in two. The barrel lay about two feet from the rest of the pistol. The gun was made of pressed sawdust and painted with beautiful western designs. Teed's heart broke with the gun barrel.

"Don't worry about that, Teed," Jake soothed. "We can tape it back on.

It'll be all right—just like new." He tried to console the distraught boy. He went to a cupboard in the kitchen and got a roll of tape.

"No, it won't," Teed called after Jake, disappointment controlling his voice. "I can't shoot as far as Gillis can if my gun has a broke barrel."

"This tape will hold the bullets straight," Jake said, coming back into the room. "Here, let me tape it back on," he offered, and using a strip of black friction tape, he made the gun look whole again.

Teed wasn't satisfied with the repairs. "I still can't shoot as far as Gillis can," he complained. "It'll fall off the first time I have to shoot it." He looked at the gun for a moment. Suddenly, his eyes lit up with a great idea. "Gillis, I'll trade you my gun and this big 'nanner for just your gun!" he bartered, holding the gun and banana out, hoping Gillis would accept. "You're little and don't need to shoot very far, and this short-barreled gun will shoot just as far as a little kid like you needs to shoot. Let's make a good swap. Then ever'body will be happy."

"No deal, Brother," Gillis said. "I'm already happy. I already have a big 'nanner—a good gun, too. Why should I give my good gun for your 'nanner and a broke gun? I'd be plumb stupid to do a thing like that." Gillis rubbed his hand over the smooth surface of his gun and smiled disdainfully at Teed, savoring the moment.

"You young 'uns wash up for breakfast," Vann called from the kitchen.

"We ain't hungry," Skatney called back, continuing to eat everything she could find in her cap.

"Come on and put the candy and stuff up till after you eat breakfast," came Vann's reply.

"Yeah, come on, Teed. You can't shoot any wild animals for your food with that broke gun," Gillis said, running to the kitchen.

There was a sumptuous repast waiting. The entire family slurped and gnyammed its way through the meal.

Afterwards, there was a discussion of each gift, of all that had happened during the past year, of the happiness of each family member. The meal had made the two little boys forget about what Santa *could* have brought if he had not shown favoritism. The presents were proof that Santa did care. The

the bicycle was forgotten for the moment.

A knock on the front door brought the family discussion to an abrupt end.

Teed went to the door and admitted three boys—Esker and Tester Seedy and Satch Hood. Each sported a new set of cap busters with western designs. Teed could smell the powder smoke from the expired caps. "Come on in, boys. Me and Gillis will be with you in a jiffy or two."

Morning chores were hurriedly taken care of, and then there ensued some wild, shoot-'em-up cowboy games.

"Let's pl'ike we're cowboys from the picture shows," Satch Hood suggested.

"Good idee. I'll be Randolph Scott," Tester said.

"I'll be Roy Rogers," Gillis added.

"I'll be Gene Autry," Esker chimed. "And Teed can be an Indian, 'cause all western shows have some Indians in 'em."

"I'm not *some* Indians. I'm a *lone* Indian," Teed laughed.

"He can be Chief Short Shot, 'cause of his short-barreled gun," Satch said, laughing at the monicker he had given Teed.

"That's all right with me, fellers," Teed grinned. "I can shoot as many bad cowboys with this short gun as you can shoot Indians with your long 'uns."

Esker and Satch went around one side of the log barn, while Tester and Gillis went around the opposite side. Each boy banged away at all-alone Teed.

Teed banged back. His make-believe bullets fell short of their target due to the damaged gun. The tape had slipped off, letting the barrel fall to the ground. He discarded the broken barrel as a lost cause. To make up for distance, Teed shot faster, hoping to down one of the fleeing cowboys. "I know I got you, Satch," he yelled as his buddy passed from view behind the barn.

"Your bullet hit about two foot behind me," Satch yelled back. "That was a short shot. Your gun's just a little too short."

"Hey, you guys, stop for just a minute and come back. Let's reorganize our plan of action," Teed called out.

"You ain't gonna shoot us when we come out of our hiding places, are you?" Esker asked from his position behind the barn.

"No, I won't," Teed assured him. "Come on out."

As everyone came into view, Teed, showing disgust and frustration, threw his gun into the hayloft. He could retrieve it later and repair it when he had more time. But right at that very moment, though, he would have to fight that cowboy and Indian conflict without a gun.

"I've changed my name to Chief Shooting Finger. I've brought a bunch of rustlers, and lots of Indians, to their knees with this trusty finger." He pointed toward the sky and yelled, "Bang!" He then blew on the end of his finger like he had seen gunslingers do in the movies. "I'm ready now," he reported, starting to chase the bad cowboys around the corner of the barn. "Bang! Bang! I got you, Esker," he shouted excitedly. He continued to run around the barn, shooting at his fleeing friends. "Bang! Bang! I know I got you that time, Esker Seedy."

Sniff and a Cherry Pie

Bunny, a beautiful little girl, caught Teed's eye one cold October day when he was a student at Coaley Creek Elementary School. The boy did not know what love and romance were, but something akin to love surely was tugging at his heart, trying to get a strong grip on him. He thought he was doing rather well in winning the pretty girl's affections. His hopes were lifted a couple of notches when her brother, Red, spoke to Teed a couple of times. Since the two boys had become such good buddies, it wouldn't be very long before Bunny would become his for keeps, Teed figured.

Teed was sitting there at his desk that October morning. He had caught a cold the night before. October can be very unpredictable. The previous morning had been warm for that time of year, and Teed, being the rough-and-tough-type fellow, had gone to school in a short-sleeved shirt. During the day, the weather had turned extremely cold; the temperature had dropped drastically. Teed had to walk the two-mile trip home without a coat. The result was a bad cold and a runny nose.

While Teed sat at his desk doing his arithmetic assignment, his nose broke loose and began to stream. Automatically he reached for the handkerchief that his mother always made sure he had. But much to his chagrin, there wasn't one in his back pocket, causing the lovesick boy to almost panic. He held his nose with his thumb and index finger and frantically searched his other pockets, hoping to find the elusive handkerchief, but to no avail.

There was nothing else to do, so he started at about his elbow, on his shirtsleeve, sniffing as he pulled his arm along under his nose. He looked to his right and two rows of seats over.

There sat pretty little Bunny. She was looking right at Teed, making the boy wonder just how long she had been staring at him. Maybe it could have been the sound he made as he wiped his nose on his sleeve that had drawn her attention his way. Anyway, she was looking at him, and that was wonderfully exciting. He swelled with pride, realizing that he was making headway on the road to a perfect love life.

Bunny made a pretty little face by wrinkling up her nose and closing her eyes.

Teed did not know whether she was making a face because she thought he had done a crude and repulsive thing or she was winking at him because she liked him. Maybe she was just learning to wink, and, being new at it, maybe she couldn't do it without closing both eyes. Whatever it was, she looked straight at him, and that was all that mattered to him. To be sure of what her eye closing meant, Teed made another run along his nose with his sleeve as an excuse to look across the aisle in Bunny's direction—sniffing louder on his second run.

Sure enough, Bunny made that same little gesture, with her nose up and eyes closed.

Teed knew that she was winking at him. Surely she would not have done the same thing twice if she had not been flirting with him. He was so elated that he could hardly wait until morning recess period to show off a little for her. Any young fellow would be more than willing to strut for Bunny. He was so shaken up by the turn of events that he could not remember the multiplication table—the *one* even. He was really disconcerted. His mind was a blank as he tried to do his assignment. Maybe if he strutted and showed off for her, she would like him even more. If strutting and showing off weren't the answer to winning her heart, he would try differently. Surely there was another way to her heart if his first effort didn't work.

Teed had four Indian-head nickels in his pocket. At lunchtime Gillis, his friend Satch, and he had planned to go to a little grocery store about a mile down the road from the schoolhouse.

Pete Moss had a one-room general store where Coaley Creek and Big Bull Creek joined forces to form Bass Creek River.

Teed had already asked the teacher, Miss Wills, and she had agreed to let the three boys make the trip to the store. Teed intended to buy something sweet for sweet Bunny, his love. Those goodies waiting patiently there in the display jars would surely win her affections. But he planned to do something at recess that would really catch her eye and prepare her for the goodies he intended to buy for her.

Finally, Miss Wills looked at her watch and announced recess period.

Teed hurried outside—the first kid out the door. He wanted to get out ahead of Bunny, to get his brogan shoes loosened up enough to be able to do some great movements. He planned to show Bunny how athletic he was. He did a few handsprings—not landing very gracefully—before Bunny and some of her friends came outside. He practiced hurriedly, preparing for Bunny's emergence from the little one-room schoolhouse.

When Teed saw Bunny with a rope in her hand, organizing the girls in a game of jump rope, he started his routine. Somersaults, handstands, handsprings, and standing on his head were the extent of his routine, except for running. He planned to try running later.

Bunny and Josie Milt began swinging the jump rope while the other little girls jumped and skipped as the rope went over their heads, then under their moving feet.

Teed could tell that Bunny was watching him, even though she had her back turned so that he couldn't see her face. He just knew that she was watching out of the corner of her eye. When she caught one of the girls under the chin with the jump rope, it was a dead giveaway. That was all that Teed needed to see to realize that he had made a big impression on that little girl.

Gillis walked by and told Teed that he was making a big fool of himself. "You'll break your fool neck trying to show your acrobatic skills just to impress Bunny," Gillis said, then went to play with a bunch of fourth-graders, leaving Teed to his strutting.

"What does a little kid know about life and love?" Teed thought. "What does he know about winning a girl's heart? Maybe when Gillis grows up as big as me, he'll know then just how I feel in my heart for Bunny." Teed talked out loud to himself. The lovelorn boy immediately forgot Gillis' words of warning.

Teed returned to his antics, his big brogans doing a number on the grass and gravels on the playground. He somersaulted, his shoes striking the ground like a beaver's tail on a still mountain pond—much louder, though. His brogans were about two sizes too large—the size his mother always bought for him, hoping they would last awhile, since the kid was growing so fast. With the workout that he was giving the shoes right then, he would be lucky to get two-weeks wear out of them.

Bunny was still watching from the corner of her eye, Teed figured, even though she was swinging the jump rope while talking and laughing with Josie Milt and the other girls.

Teed attempted to do a handstand while keeping his eyes on Bunny. It just so happened that there was a thistle plant right where he put his left hand. The sharp spines pierced his palm, causing him to wince with pain. His right arm wasn't strong enough to hold all of his weight as he tried to lift his left hand off the thistle to get a little relief. Losing his balance, he went down, landing on his face in the grass and gravels—mostly gravels. Rising slowly to a sitting position, he looked around to see if anyone was watching. No one was, except Bunny, maybe. Teed was almost sure that she was watching him from the corner of her eye. He knew that she could not keep her eyes off him while he did his antics.

Bunny was bent over tying her sneakers and missed the action.

Oh, no! Josie Milt was watching. He certainly hoped that he had not done enough to impress her. She was that big girl who hit him on the shoulder so hard when he was in the first grade. That unforgettable frog that had popped up on his arm so many years ago seemed to be kicking and thrashing around in his memory, still trying to jump off his skinny arm.

Teed got to his feet very slowly and began to pick the thistle spines out of his dirty hand. When he finished doing that, he began a cleanup of his dirty, scratched face. He dug three good-sized gravels out of his forehead, causing blood to ooze from his punctured brow. When he wiped the back of his hand across his forehead in an attempt to dislodge more gravels and dirt, he felt something wet. Giving his hand a quick perusal, he found a trace of real blood. His heart thumped excitedly as he ran around Bunny and the other girls as they continued to jump rope. Surely Bunny would see the blood on his face and realize that he was a very tough kid.

When the boy figured that he had done just enough to get all the girls' attention, especially Bunny's, he revved up his brogan shoes another notch to get the needed rpms, then raced across the playground at breakneck speed, and it was almost that, literally. He was looking back to see if Bunny was watching, when suddenly he stopped. He did not realize that he was so close to the basketball goalpost. He made a sudden, unscheduled stop. What a stop!

Teed fell backward and landed on the hard ground, his head striking the rough surface of the basketball court. He landed with a star-spangled thud. An astronomer could have picked out several constellations from that group of stars orbiting his head.

It doesn't take a big event to draw a huge crowd. Most of the students saw Teed's collision with the post and ran to investigate.

Teed looked up through that moving haze of stars and saw numerous pairs of eyes staring down at him. Each pair of eyes had a big wide-opened mouth under it that sent many roars of laughter down at the embarrassed boy. He lay there on the hard ground for a while, trying to get his senses back and to get control over his body muscles before attempting to rise and dash away at full speed. He wasn't ready to give up in his quest to impress Bunny. Gradually he rose to his feet—very slowly at first—and just as he bounded away toward the other end of the playground at a sprinter's speed, the bell rang to end the recess period. It was a good thing for Teed. He could not have lasted very much longer, the way he had expended his energy.

No one asked if the collision with the goalpost hurt. Everyone just laughed.

Teed was all right. It's very hard to hurt a lad in love. He came out of that little incident unscathed. He did all that he possibly could for Bunny's attention. He made a big hit with the little girl, he thought. Actually, he made two hits—one with Bunny, the other with that goalpost. "Just let that little sweet tater wait till lunchtime!" he muttered to himself. "I'll make my sure-to-win pitch with a big bag of goodies." That store down the road would be his aid in winning sweet Bunny's love.

*   *   *   *

Teed, Gillis, and Satch Hood headed for the store at lunchtime. They ran nearly all the way to the fork of Blue Domer and Coaley creeks.

Teed filled a big bag with sweets for Bunny. Bubble gum, gumdrops, different flavored candy wrapped in cellophane, a pack of regular chewing gum, and suckers made up the selection. Those four nickels bought a big bag of wooing goodies.

Gillis bought a cherry pie with his nickel. One nickel was all that he had.

Maybe Teed should have shared his money with Gillis, but he didn't. He spent his money on someone else. There was no sharing of his sweets with a boy, not even Gillis, and Gillis was his kith and kin.

The trio walked along, in no hurry to get back to the classroom.

Gillis and Satch opened their goodies and began to eat.

Teed didn't eat any of his. Everything that he had purchased was for sweet little Bunny.

Gillis was having a problem with his pie. He could hardly swallow after having chewed on one bite for a long time. His eyes seemed to almost glaze and set back in his head as he tried to swallow that cantankerous piece of pie. The pie must have had grippers by the way it clung to his throat. The kid resembled a chickey-diddle trying to swallow a corn bread crust that was too big.

Teed watched Gillis trying to eat the tough pie. "Was that Gillis' neck squeaking?" he wondered as the tough pie went down. A drink of cold water or pop—anything—would help wash the pie on down to the stomach. He felt sorry for his brother, but there was nothing he could do. There was no water to offer to help wash the pie on down.

"I don't like this pie," Gillis croaked. "Would either of you all want it? If you don't, and I can't blame you if you don't, I'm gonna throw it in the creek," he threatened, aiming for the stream that flowed parallel with the narrow road.

Teed wanted the pie, but he wouldn't take it. He didn't want to share his goodies with Gillis. If he took the pie, Gillis would expect something in return.

"I'll take it if you don't want it," Satch said, accepting the offer.

Gillis handed the pie to Satch and watched as his friend removed it from the paper plate in which it was packed and began to eat.

"This is a real good pie," Satch mumbled through a mouthful.

Teed looked at the paper plate that Satch threw on the ground. Part of it was gone, and teeth marks were on the remaining part. Gillis had been eating the paper plate along with the pie.

"You're a nut, Gillis! Don't you know enough to remove the pie from the plate before you start eating?" Teed asked. "You sure must have been hungry to start eating before you got it out of its wrapper. Why didn't you look at it closer? Satch sure performed a good disappearing act with your cherry pie."

"I didn't know that it was in a paper plate," Gillis whined. "It was the same color as the pie crust."

"That sure was good," Satch beamed, licking the pie filling off his fingers.

"Give me some of your stuff, Teed," Gillis begged. "If you don't give me part of yours, I'll tell Dad that you wouldn't share with me." He looked like he was ready to cry.

"Go ahead and tell, and I'll tell him that you ate a paper plate," Teed laughed. "I don't want to impress you. I just want to impress Bunny and get her to like me a lot better."

"Bunny won't like you any more than she does now, even if you do give her all that candy and chewing gum," Gillis continued to complain.

"She can't like me much more than she does right now," Teed said, boasting. "She's already crazy about me, and I've not even given her the candy and chewing gum that I bought for her."

"Yeah, she's crazy all right—that is if she likes anyone like you!" Gillis stormed.

"Here's a piece of candy bar, Gillis." Satch made an offering of the remainder of his confection. "You give me a pie, and the least I can do for you is share my candy with you."

"Thanks, Satch," Gillis said, showing his appreciation for the gesture of kindness. "You like me more than that hateful brother of mine does."

"Not really. I just swapped the candy for the pie," Satch said, opening another candy bar.

"I'm sure that that statement made you feel good, Gillis," Teed snickered.

There was no reply from Gillis. He sulked along in silence. He surely was a mad kid.

The bell ending lunchtime rang before the boys reached the schoolhouse. They hurried to get there before classes began.

"You fellows are late," Miss Wills said, reprimanding the boys for their tardiness.

"I'm sorry," Teed apologized. "Gillis had some trouble with a cherry pie." He smiled and looked at Gillis. The little boy was still mad.

"Don't ask me to let you go again," she stated. "You have lost that privilege."

"Miss Wills," Josie Milt blurted out, raising her hand and snapping her fingers together to get attention.

"Yes, Josie, what do you want now?" Miss Wills asked.

"Someone has been cutting on the basketball goalpost," she began. "And I believe they tried to draw a cow or something on it," she continued, tattling on someone.

"That was Teed Cornfield that done it," Buck Skyler reported.

Buck was a big boy, almost sixteen years old and only in the fourth grade. He was a slow learner, and mean. His parents sent him to school just to get rid of him during the day so they would not have to contend with his meanness at home.

"Teed *did* it," Miss Wills said, correcting Buck's grammar.

"I did not, Miss Wills!" Teed snapped. "Don't accuse me of it!"

"I didn't mean that you did it," Miss Wills said, smiling pleasantly. "I was only correcting Buck."

"I didn't draw a picture on that goalpost!" Teed retorted. "I didn't cut on it, either. I don't want to be accused of something that I didn't do." Teed was hot under the collar and showing it.

"Miss Wills," Buck continued his moment of fun, "Teed was trying to show off for Bunny. That was when he run and hit that post." When Buck got something started, he carried it as far as he could. "His teeth cut that post," he continued, "and he had some money in his pocket. He hit that post so hard that he made an imprint of a buffalo with one of his nickels."

Teed bowed his head so no one could see his face as everyone laughed at his embarrassment. He couldn't face his friends.

"There was no point in bringing that up, Buck. Teed didn't do any damage to that goalpost," Miss Wills said.

Her words helped lift Teed's spirits a little. At least she didn't make such a big deal of his efforts to impress Bunny.

"It's the truth, Miss Wills," Buck said, a big grin splitting his ugly face.

"I just thought that you might want to know all about what happened," Josie added.

"Well, just for your information, young lady, and you, too, Buck, you didn't have to tell me about it," Miss Wills stated. "Now, let's leave Teed alone and start studying." She turned to the blackboard to write the assignments for the afternoon.

Everyone laughed because Miss Wills put Josie Milt in her place, again.

Teed hid the bag of goodies in his desk and began to study his history assignment, without looking at pretty Bunny again until evening recess.

Teed was the last person to leave the room when Miss Wills announced recess. He went straight to the goalpost to see if Buck and Josie were right about the evidence of his collision with it. There were some gouge marks about the height his mouth reached on the post when he stood up straight, but anything could have made those marks. Lower down on the post was a faint imprint of something that could have been that of a buffalo, if one had a good imagination and viewed it at a certain angle. He had hit that post pretty hard and at a high rate of speed. After a thorough inspection of the evidence, he went in search of Bunny. He found her with her friends, jumping rope, and gave her the candy.

Bunny took the bag and kissed Teed on the cheek, saying, "Thank you, Teed Cornfield."

Teed blushed and raced away as fast as he could, but not before he heard Bunny say, "I'd kiss any type of monkey for this much candy and chewing gum."

Bunny laughed along with the other girls and shared the goodies with them.

Teed's gesture of love had not meant anything to that pretty little girl. He had spent his money and used all his energy for nothing. Even though Bunny had proven to be fickle, Teed began to plan a new strategy to woo her love. He would continue his love-quest, for that little put-down was nothing to worry about.

Hainted Candy

Teed had just returned to his seat after morning recess that warm May morning at Coaley Creek Elementary School. Satch Hood sat in the seat in front of Teed, and Gillis sat in the fourth grade row, across the aisle.

The three boys continued to talk about something that had happened during recess. They did not cease talking until they heard Josie Milt ask the teacher a question.

"Mr. Banner, why are you writing names on the blackboard?" she asked. "They're all boys' names." When she received no answer to her first question, she asked another one. She could ask more questions than anyone could answer. "Why haven't you written some of the girls' names up there on the blackboard with the boys' names?"

Mr. Banner continued to write names on the board, paying no attention to nosey Josie Milt.

"It's 'cause us boys are much better than you girls," Satch Hood said, laughing, turning to Teed for approval of the wisecrack.

Teed liked the little joke, laughing to show it.

The rest of the students laughed with the two boys—all except Josie Milt.

Josie sulked and tossed her head in an effort to sling her long, straight, corn silk-colored hair out of her face. She looked at Teed and Satch with a surliness that could have clabbered milk.

"It's because we're so good," Josie snapped. "The girls don't get into as much trouble as you boys do is why he doesn't write our names up there. You boys are in a lot a trouble, I believe."

Teed, Gillis, and Satch continued to laugh at Satch's joke—that boys were better than girls. They ignored Josie Milt.

Josie Milt tried continuously to get the boys into trouble, and most of the girls, too. She had very few friends. Her attitude and temperament were the reasons for her lack of popularity with the other students. They simply could not stand her.

Mr. Banner looked out over the room at all the curious faces, then turned back to the blackboard to write another name on it—another boy's name.

"Mr. Tedder, the teacher over at Big Bull Creek Elementary School, has invited us to play a game of ball," Mr. Banner began to explain, but he was drowned out by the roar of the cheering students. When the yelling finally ceased, he began anew. "I have the names of nine players and three substitutes listed," he said, pointing to the blackboard. "I want you to play hard and to show good sportsmanship during the game. If you can control your emotions, you will do just fine. Even though you may not agree with a call by the umpire, be a good sport and accept the decision and cooperate with the official. If you can do that, you will be winners in more ways than by just scoring runs. Are there any questions?"

"Yeah. When can we get started, Mr. Banner?" Satch Hood asked.

"In a few minutes, Satch," Mr. Banner replied. "I want you to be the team captain. Teed Cornfield can be co-captain. Teed can help you to keep the team in line. You two fellows will have to be prime examples for the rest of the players."

"You can count on me, Mr. Banner," Teed beamed, assuring the teacher that he would be more than glad to help keep the team in line.

"Are you going to let some of us girls go along to say cheers for the team?" Josie queried.

"No, he's not," Teed retorted. "We don't need any cheering done for us. We can play better without the likes of you along, acting silly and insulting people."

The boys agreed with Teed, cheering his remark, laughing and pointing to Josie Milt, who sat in her seat and sulked.

"This bickering among yourselves won't be necessary, students," Mr. Banner stated. "Satch, give this to Mr. Tedder," he said, handing Satch an envelope addressed to the Big Bull Creek teacher. "There is a letter and a lineup of the players in the envelope. Mr. Tedder will place each of you at your respective positions from the instructions I have written in here." He pointed to the envelope.

"Do you want me and Satch to read it as we go along and plan our strategy by placing the players in their positions?" Teed asked. "We know where each kid plays best. You ain't out on the playing field with us all the time, so me and Satch know more about who plays best at what position. We know more about that than you do, Mr. Banner."

"My instructions will be sufficient, Teed," Mr. Banner said, smiling, amused with Teed's statement. "Just give the envelope to Mr. Tedder. He will take care of the lineup."

"That will put you in your place, know-it-all Teed Cornfield," Josie Milt sneered, turning to the other students for their support in her efforts to embarrass Teed. Glaring stares from the other students caused her to turn back to the front of the room. She received a stern reprimand from the teacher.

"Josie, that will be enough from you," Mr. Banner told her.

The boys took Josie's reprimand as an opportunity to chide her more.

The students could have continued the controversy among themselves, but Mr. Banner let them know who was in charge. The room quieted to only meek smiles.

"When can we get started toward Big Bull Creek, Mr. Banner?" Teed asked impatiently.

"As soon as I call the roll," Mr. Banner stated. "As I call each player's name, come to the front of the room and line up along the wall behind my desk. Satch, you and Teed come on up here. I want you to be ready to lead the team to victory."

"All right!" Teed yelled, jumping to his feet. He skipped to the front of the room and stood there with a thistle-eating grin while the teacher read the names of the rest of the team.

Gillis was the last name on the list, and with his bringing up the rear, the team left the room with a whoop of excitement.

Teed could hear Josie Milt protesting Mr. Banner's decision not to send the girls along as cheerleaders. "I know that we could make a difference,

Mr. Banner," were the last words Teed heard as he and the rest of the team left the building and hurried toward Big Bull Creek Elementary School, on the other side of the mountain.

* * * *

Teed and the feisty ball team from Coaley Creek arrived at Big Bull Creek Elementary School at noon.

The Big Bull Creek students stopped their playing and talking and watched the visitors' approach to the crowded school yard.

With a few "howdys" and many back pats, the visitors were instantaneous friends as they mingled about, speaking to the home team, getting better acquainted.

The Big Bull students were aware of the proposed game. A little girl ran to inform Mr. Tedder of the arrival of the Coaley Creek team, and immediately preparations were commenced to organize a baseball game.

The playing field was a vacant lot about fifty feet wide by one hundred feet long, between the highway and Big Bull Creek, the little stream from which the community got its name.

Josie Milt had a good point about the cheerleaders accompanying the team. The cheering section for the Big Bull players was the entire school enrollment.

When one of the Coaley Creek players was at bat, the noise was so deafening that the batter was confused and had a difficult time getting a good hit, but they did very well, considering the circumstances. No one remembered the exact score or number of innings played, but when the game was over, and if his memory served him right, Teed figured that the game lasted about three innings and three hours, with a tie score of about ninety-one to ninety-one.

Everyone had a good time, and after many good-byes, handshakes, and shoulder punches—with pop-up frogs the results—Teed and his team reluctantly started their long journey back to Coaley Creek. The hot sun bore down on them unmercifully as they plodded along the dusty road, in no great hurry to reach their destination before time for school to be dismissed for the day.

* * * *

A worn-out bunch of boys arrived back on Coaley Creek about half an hour before time to go home. They were no longer the feisty, energetic team that left that same building earlier in the day.

There were no excited boys and girls to greet them as they had anticipated. Upon entering the empty building, they were met by complete silence, causing them to wonder where everyone had gone.

"What's that?" Gillis asked, pointing toward the wall behind the teacher's desk.

Everyone ran to see what Gillis had found.

There was a large paper bag sitting on the floor—up against the wall.

"Open that paper poke up and take a look in it," Teed suggested. "Let us know the secret of its contents. It could be a haint trap, you know. You boys know that this schoolhouse is haunted, don't you?"

"You know better than that, Teed," Jubal Cornfield said, sniffing loudly, rubbing a shirtsleeve under his runny nose—a disgusting habit.

"Tell them why it's hainted, Satch," Teed said, turning to Satch Hood.

"Yeah, it's hainted here all right—at night, that is," Satch said, beginning to relate the story about the haunted schoolhouse.

"What's in there?" Teed asked, stepping forward to open the bag to inspect its contents, interupting Satch's story.

There it was, a huge bag—almost full of candy. There were peppermint sticks, horehound sticks, loose pieces of all-flavored candy, and on the very top there were pieces of candy shaped like ocean waves, the likes of which none of the boys had ever seen before.

Teed figured that a "haint" had melted the pieces of candy and made them look like the waves on the ocean, just to scare the person who might want to eat some of it.

"Satch, have you ever seen anything like that?" Teed asked, bewildered by the presence of the odd-shaped candy in the brown bag.

"No, I've not, Teed," Satch replied. "Haints don't usually come out in the daytime. The only reason they came out today is because everyone was away and the room was empty. A haint placed the candy here as a decoy to lure some innocent child away to haint land with him."

All Teed could see around him were open mouths and eyeballs. The boys were scared stiff with the thoughts of "haints" in the schoolhouse.

Gillis finally gained enough composure and courage to ask a question. "Why is there a haint in this old schoolhouse anyway? How did one get in here to stay?"

"Satch, tell Gillis and the rest of the boys how the haint got in here," Teed suggested. He had heard the story many times, but he wanted Satch to tell it, since Satch's folks were akin to the slain man who supposedly became the ghost.

"My dad's great uncle—on his father's side of the family—was playing cards with a bunch of other men right here under this building," Satch said, relating the much-told story. "Whiskey was going around amongst the card players, as well as a bunch of other men standing around watching the game. Boys, whiskey was the main reason for Uncle Thadius Hood's death. Jude Wheddle, a friend of my great, great uncle's, got crazy-mad 'cause Uncle Thadius got the last drink in the bottle. So he up and stobbed Uncle Thadius with a hawk-billed pocketknife. They say that it went all the way to the holler part of his belly, and Uncle Thadius was too drunk to fight back. He died right here under this schoolhouse. Now that's what rotten whiskey will do to people when they drink it. I'll never drink the stuff when I grow up. I don't want to get stobbed all the way to the holler part of my belly by a drunk man with a long-bladed pocketknife. That sure would be a horrible way to die. The story goes that Uncle Thadius bled so much that the entire dirt floor was covered with his blood. I don't know if that is true or not, but that's what's allus been told about why the haint's in the shoolhouse."

"He couldn't bleed that much. He didn't have enough blood to cover the entire floor," Gillis argued. "He would have to have a hundred gallons of blood in him to bleed that much, and I know that nobody, big or little, could have a hundred gallons of blood in him. If he did, you could hear him sloshing a mile away as he walked down the road."

"Yeah, I know it," Satch continued. "But they say that the blood can still be seen on the ground when the coal is used up."

"Has the coal ever been used up before?" Gillis wanted to know.

"Not that I know of," Satch admitted.

"Well, you don't know if the blood's still there or not," Gillis told him.

"Well, that's what I've allus heard," Satch went on.

"That ain't what I just heard," Teed yelled, running for the door, followed by eleven screaming boys.

After everyone had exited the building, Teed, laughing at his hood-winked friends, saw Mr. Banner and the rest of the students coming up the road toward the schoolhouse.

"How did the game go, fellows?" Mr. Banner asked as he arrived at the schoolhouse, where the athletes were horsing around.

"It was a tie," Teed reported. "The score was about ninety-one to ninety-one, I think. You would have been proud of us—the way we played that Big Bull Creek team. Today was one of our best games. Our defense was just a little tad off, but our offense was super."

"Mr. Banner," Josie Milt began, "if you had let some of us girls go along with the team, we could have cheered them on to a victory."

"You probably would have caused a fight," Teed growled. "We did very well without you and we're proud of our success. We'd probably have lost if you'd been there to distract us."

"You might have won if we had been there to support you," Josie argued, continuing to chide the boys for their failure to win the game.

"We did just fine without you," Teed declared.

"You didn't do well enough by yourselves to win," Josie said, slinging her long hair in an effort to get it out of her face.

"Mr. Banner, the haints have been at work while you were away from the schoolhouse," Gillis said, ignoring Josie Milt's remark. "They put out some hexed candy to use as bait to lure some unsuspecting kids to haint land."

"There aren't any ghosts in the schoolhouse, and that candy was put there by Josie's uncle. He is on leave from the Army. While we were on our field trip, we met Bradley Milt on the road. He said that he would leave the candy in the schoolhouse for Josie."

"We could have had some of that candy," Gillis whined, showing regret. "You said that it was hainted, Teed."

"We can still have some of it," Teed said, then raced toward the schoolhouse. He was just a little too late.

Josie Milt climbed the steps to the building. She would soon take possession of the "hainted" candy.

Sing for the Super

Teed stood at the front of the room that morning at Coaley Creek Elementary School. He looked at the many faces staring back at him. A song ran through his mind. It ran through all right—straight through and out into space—gone. He couldn't remember the words to it, and he wanted to remember them so he could belt it out to his eager audience. He always jumped at the chance to get up in front of the room and sing a song, especially the one about a dilapidated old log house—his favorite.

Each Friday, Teed, along with the rest of the students, was given the opportunity to sing his way to Coaley Creek greatness by staging a talent contest.

The teacher, Miss Wright, enjoyed listening to the students' screeching and squalling—what they called singing. She seemed to enjoy it, since she often let them begin their talent contest, then left the room to listen at a distance. She said that their singing, heard from a distance, was much better, more soothing to her very sensitive eardrums.

Teed stood there in front of the room, wracking his brain, trying to find the right tune and the right pitch. The words seemed to play hide-and-seek with him, preventing his getting started. He hummed several bars but could not catch the words as they swam—splashed about—in an unorganized state through his brain. He couldn't remember that song entitled "That Precious Little Log House of Childhood Memories That Stood on the Hill Above My Son's House Where I Live Now." That was a long title to a short song. If he could remember the title, maybe he could remember the words to the entire song. He should. There were very few extra words to remember. His mind was blank, though. He grunted and snorted a few times, scuffed his foot on the floor, trying his best to remember. Finally, he gave up. He sat down and lost the contest as gracefully as the situation would allow. He bowed his head and listened, in silence.

Esker Seedy won the contest with a song that he had written entitled "Goin' Frog Giggin'." The song told a story of how Esker and his brothers went out at night to gig frogs for a frog-leg fry.

The song was pretty good, but it did not have as much good meaning to it as the song that Teed had planned to sing but forgot the words to. Teed was so sad that he lost the contest.

During lunch everyone was with Esker Seedy, patting him on the back and congratulating him on his feat of dethroning Teed Cornfield from the high seat of class crooner.

"You sure messed up your long-titled song," Tester Seedy reminded Teed for the hundredth time. "You sure did fire a blank! If I couldn't do any better than that, I'd just up and quit." He walked on by, laughing at dejected Teed.

Esker, Tester, and Satch Hood, Teed's best friends, were walking around with their arms around one another's necks, like good friends will do. Even Gillis was right behind them as they walked around, trying to sing about gigging frogs. Esker was the only one who knew the words, but Tester, Satch, and Gillis got a word in now and then. They yelled and mumbled until they came to a word they remembered, then yelled that word as loud as they could. They couldn't even carry a tune, but that didn't matter much to them. They were having a great time. There was one thing for certain: that bunch needed singing lessons. They croaked around and made a big racket.

"Gillis, why are you stabbing me in the back by squalling and grunting around with that bunch?" Teed asked his brother as the boys passed on one of their many trips around the schoolhouse. "I'm your kith and kin. Come and be with me." He stood there all alone and watched the four boys as they passed him by.

"Teed, I'd rather be with a winner," Gillis called over his shoulder as the four singers turned the corner of the building and passed from sight.

Their squawking was still audible to Teed, even though the boys were behind the corner of the building.

As the quartet came back into view, Teed saw Esker Seedy thrusting an imaginary gig at an imaginary frog. The other boys aped his actions, thrusting their imaginary gigs at the air.

"You can laugh and make fun of my failure, and just the one time have I failed to put down anyone who has ever challenged me to a singing duel," Teed called to the noisy boys as they passed. "When we go in after lunch, you backbiters can rest assured that I will put all of you under the table with a song that I have just written. I'll have to tell you the story behind it to make it simple enough for you knuckleheads to understand it."

The four lads passed on by, paying no attention to Teed's words of warning. They continued to sing and thrust their imaginary gig poles at the air.

"You're having fun right now, but just you wait until you hear my new song!" Teed yelled, disgusted with the jubilant boys singing about a bullfrog.

After the bell rang, ending the lunch hour, Teed marched into the classroom and sat down with the rest of the students.

"Miss Wright," Josie Milt called out over the noise of the children as they settled into their seats. "Teed Cornfield said that he didn't have a chance to win the singing contest this morning. He says that he has a new song that he wrote in order to reclaim his title from Esker Seedy."

"We won't have time for any more singing today," Miss Wright informed nosey Josie Milt.

"Please, Miss Wright," Josie begged, "let Teed sing his new song so we can compare it to Esker Seedy's frog-gigging song."

"Maybe we can do that tomorrow. We need to review for our history test that is coming up soon," Miss Wright said, answering Josie Milt.

"But this is Friday, Miss Wright," Josie protested, slinging her long hair out of her face from force of habit. "We don't have school tomorrow."

"We need the review anyway," Miss Wright replied. "Maybe some of the information will stay with you over the weekend. I doubt if it will, but I hope it does. Sit down."

As the room quieted down, and all the moaning and groaning ended, Teed looked out the window and saw a new car as it pulled up to the building and stopped.

A car was a novelty to the folks on Coaley Creek. Very few people in that area had automobiles. If a person was lucky enough to own a car, it was usually parked most of the time due to two or three flat tires or an empty gas tank.

Teed's father often said that it was easier and cheaper to keep his horse full of hay and corn than it was to keep a car full of gas.

"Who's that man getting out of that big new car?" Josie Milt asked. She had noticed Teed looking out the window, and since she was the nosiest person to ever inhabit this wonderful green earth, she had to check to see what the boy was looking at.

The entire class ran to the window, jockeying for a position to look at the stranger in the new car.

"Who is it, Teed?" Gillis asked, but got no answer. "Who is it, Teed?" he asked a second time. He still got no answer.

"Children, sit down!" Miss Wright ordered. She had to shout to be heard. "That is Mr. Cus, the school superintendent. He is here to visit with us. Now, sit down and be nice and quiet when he enters the room."

Hurriedly, but not quietly, the children returned to their seats. A few books were knocked to the floor, some on purpose, as everyone hastened to obey Miss Wright's order. They were sitting as straight as rows of cornstalks in a field when Mr. Cus knocked on the door and quietly entered the room.

"Now, students . . ." Miss Wright said, beginning an unprepared sentence. "Oh, Mr. Cus! Come in. We weren't expecting you. Come in," she stammered, trying desperately to keep from stepping on her lower lip, which had dropped almost to her ankles as the superintendent entered the room. "This certainly is a pleasant surprise."

"No, don't let me stop whatever you were doing," Mr. Cus said when Miss Wright rose and offered him a seat. "Go ahead. I will find a seat and observe your class." He tiptoed quietly to the back of the room, the students' heads turning as he passed, and took a seat behind Jubal Cornfield.

Jubal sniffed and grinned at the superintendent. He nodded his head at the man but did not speak.

Teed did not know how pleasant the unannounced visit was, but he did know that it was a big surprise for Miss Wright.

"Pour on the sugar and 'lasses," Esker Seedy whispered, none to quietly, to Satch Hood.

"What was that?" Miss Wright asked, turning toward the students, Esker Seedy in particular. She welcomed the opportunity to speak to the class. She was so unprepared and nervous due to the school superintendent's unannounced visit to Coaley Creek.

"I said it is nice to have Mr. Cus visit us and that we welcome him to hear our singing program that we have planned for the evening," Esker replied, grinning sheepishly, looking around the room for the other students' approval of his statement.

"Yes, welcome to our singing program, Mr. Cus," everyone said in a droll, sing-song invitation.

Miss Wright was taken by surprise, unable to find words to either agree or deny that the plans were legitimate. "Yes, Mr. Cus, we hope you enjoy our Coaley Creek talent," she said, a mask of frustration clouding her pleasant face.

"Bring on the talent and show me how well you can sing," Mr. Cus invited, doing his best to help the nervous teacher to relax.

"We will hear from Esker Seedy first," Miss Wright announced. "Come on, Esker. Give us your frog-gigging song."

Everyone applauded as Esker got to his feet and lumbered awkwardly to the front of the room.

Teed hoped hope on top of hope that Esker would be nervous with Mr. Cus there.

Esker wasn't the least bit timid. He seemed to be relaxed with the superintendent looking on. Surprisingly, Esker liked an audience. He started the song, his premature baritone voice squeaking and croaking with the change that comes with adolescence.

Everyone laughed at Esker's singing, and he, along with Mr. Cus and Miss Wright, thought that the students were laughing at the humor of the song. They were wrong. The students were laughing at that uncultured voice.

Finally, after what seemed like an hour of screaming and squalling, the song ended.

Teed felt that Mr. Cus was pleased with the end of all that screeching and caterwauling.

The superintendent did not show the discomforting effects of the noise beating his eardrums. He probably wanted to be nice to Esker; he applauded along with the rest of the audience.

Esker went back to his seat, sat down, and smiled his thanks to the class, Mr. Cus, and Miss Wright. He did not receive the same raucous ovation which he had enjoyed that morning. Maybe it was because company was present, a rarity on Coaley Creek, or maybe they were expecting a great song from Teed.

"Teed! Teed! Teed!" the room roared. "Give us Teed Cornfield!"

"Boo, Teed! Boo, Teed!" Esker, Tester, and Zel Seedy shouted in response to Teed's turn in front of the room with his new song.

"Children!" Miss Wright exclaimed. "We must have silence!"

Teed looked at Gillis to check his reaction. His brother wasn't booing, but he could have been.

Gillis was smiling as if nothing had happened. His face had an expression which wasn't true support, though.

"Go ahead and side with Esker, Tester, and Zel Seedy," he whispered to Gillis across the aisle. "I don't care a bit. Maybe after you hear my new song you'll come to your senses. You just like that old frog-gigging song is all."

Gillis paid no attention to Teed's complaining. He was still a youngster and could be misled by other people—until he was old enough to understand that his brother could sing better than Esker Seedy.

"Come on, Teed Cornfield," Mr. Cus invited. "I hope you have penned a good song."

"I wrote it, Mr. Cus," Teed replied, walking to the front of the room.

"Wrote…penned…whichever you want to call it," Mr. Cus returned. A broad smile was a good indication that he enjoyed Teed's reply.

"If Cousin Jubal will come up here and help me, I'll attempt to do justice to 'That Precious Little Log House of Childhood Memories That Stood on the Hill Above My Son's House Where I Live Now,'" Teed announced.

"We want your new song, Teed," Satch Hood requested, clapping his hands and whistling through his teeth.

"Yes, Teed, your new song," Josie Milt echoed. "Please, Teed, just for me."

The room roared with laughter. Everyone knew that Teed disliked Josie Milt.

Surely that little incident would not shake Teed up so much that his chance to best Esker Seedy in song would be ruined again.

Cousin Jubal went to the front of the room, grinning and sniffing, while Teed cleared his throat, preparing to sing his song.

"Now we should hear some good sniffing and grunting," Gillis said, causing the room to buzz with laughter.

Teed sang a verse of his song in a shrill, high-tenor voice. A cat with its tail caught in a barn door could not reach a higher octave than Teed was putting out. Cousin Jubal went even higher than Teed did as he repeated, "On the hill," after Teed sang the line first.

Cousin Jubal repeated the first two lines, after Teed sang them first. He then sang harmony on the rest of the chorus.

When the long-titled song ended, the classroom showed its approval with a resounding round of applause.

"We cannot use that response in competition, since Jubal helped Teed," Miss Wright said. "He will have to sing a solo to be able to compete with Esker. Do you have a solo to perform for us, Teed?"

"Teed just wanted to sing that long-titled song to get his singing box all cranked up for his new song," Satch Hood quipped. "He don't want to flub his dub when he sings his new song."

"Yeah, that's just what he done," Jubal agreed, returning to his seat. He continued to sniff in that obnoxious way and grin at the other students as if he had done something great.

"Let Teed sing his new song," Josie Milt requested once more. That time she did not say, "Please, Teed, just for me."

"Yes, the new song!" came a unanimous plea.

"Quiet! Quiet!" Miss Wright interjected. "We must control ourselves. I know that you are excited, but we must try to control ourselves. Remember, Mr. Cus, our superintendent, is with us."

"We're sorry, Miss Wright," everyone said in that droll, sing-song tone in which students are taught to respond.

Teed stood at the front of the room after Cousin Jubal returned to his seat. "Miss Wright, I have a good solo to sing for you," he said, grinning.

"Let's hear it then," the teacher snapped.

"Mr. Cus, Miss Wright, and my fellow students," he began, as he had heard speakers do, but was cut short by Gillis.

"How formal can you get, Teed?" Gillis asked. "We're just folks. You don't have to get formal with us."

"Children! Children! Quiet!" Miss Wright pleaded, attempting to get control of the class and restore order. "Remember, Mr. Cus is present."

Mr. Cus sat there with a broad smile, showing his fine bridge work. He seemed to be enjoying the situation that the teacher had fallen into.

When the room was quiet once more, Miss Wright went on. "Teed, continue. And I hope we don't have any more disturbances. Teed, continue."

"As I started to say awhile ago, I have a new song. I'll have to tell you a little story that was the subject for my song. Dad was building a coal tipple for Rusty Spiker," Teed began. "Most of you all know Rusty Spiker, I'm sure. You do, don't you?"

"Yeah. We know him," Esker Seedy said.

"Good." About ever'body knows him," Teed went on. "Well, there was this little boy with him at work one day. I got to go to work with Dad that day, too. Dad takes me with him ever' once in a while. Now, Rusty's got a milk bucket full of money and is real accommodating with it. He's real good to Bobby. Rusty buys all kinds of good things for him, like pop and cakes, and stuff like bologna, cheese, and 'matoes to make samiges out of."

Teed enjoyed telling the students about the many things which Rusty Spiker did for that little boy. He enjoyed seeing their eyes light up as he mentioned the foods that Rusty bought for that kid. He knew that each student would like to be that little boy in order to get a bunch of goodies.

"The little boy's name was Bobby." Teed continued his story about the idea for his song. "Bobby Yampton Jerzee was his full name. Now, Bobby called a 'pop' a 'dope.' Why? I don't know that. He wanted a pop—or a 'dope' as he called it—and a cake. He said that he wanted a dope and a drink 'stead of a dope and a cake. He had a dime cake, but he called it a cake-dime. He just got all mixed up in what he wanted to say was all. That happens to me sometimes, and I'm sure that you have said things back'ards before, too. Now, when Rusty Spiker asked Bobby what kind of samige he wanted, Bobby said, 'I'd rather have bologna than cheese.' Now, the song was right there in front of me. All I had to do was add some words here and there to fill in the blank spaces and to rhyme with the other words. So here is my new song, entitled 'Little Bobby Yam Jerzee.'"

In a high-tenor voice, Teed sang his song, without written music, of course.

"Oh little Bobby Yam Jerzee, cake-dime, dope-drink

Patty pullet-man

Came around the Coaley schoolhouse.

As he came around the bend,

He met a settin' hen.

It grabbed him by his ears and pulled him down.

It started peckin' on his head.

He wished that he was dead.

He said, 'I'd rather have bologna than cheese,

So get this settin' hen off of me.'

Yodel-lay-de-heeeeeeeeeee."

Teed finished the song with a resounding yodel, which was the norm for ending his songs. He bowed to Mr. Cus, Miss Wright, then to his friends. He stood there before the class and waited for the applause.

Mr. Cus was smiling, while the room was so quiet that the only sound Teed could hear was Cousin Jubal sniffing.

The students looked at one another with blank faces. Then, after a period of silence—after the song had time to sink in—the room roared with a raucous round of applause, led by the superintendent himself.

"Very good! Very good! Well done!" Miss Wright said, quickly rising from her seat. She gave Teed a nudge that sent him stumbling toward his desk.

Teed sat down in his seat, sporting a big thistle-eating grin.

Everyone liked the song. After having heard it the first time, they were hooked on it.

*   *   *   *

Everywhere Teed went on the playgrounds, after the introduction of his new song that Friday afternoon, he heard kids singing the lyrics. They were trying to sing Teed's hit song, even though they couldn't carry a tune in a number three washtub. Teed was one happy boy. Hearing the kids singing his song made his chest swell with pride. Teed Cornfield, he realized, was once again the best singer in Coaley Creek Elementary School.

Rusty Hands and Crooked Nose

To Teed Cornfield, it seemed only a short time since last Halloween, and here it was again.

"That boy's growing like a horseweed," Teed's father often said.

Teed was spiking right on up, growing out of his clothes faster than his parents could find replacements for them. His pants looked as if they were expecting high water, and his shirtsleeves seemed to be ashamed of his hands as they inched their way toward his elbows.

Halloween for the people on Coaley Creek was very simple. There were only a few things that Teed and the other kids could do for excitement, except for dressing up in a crazy costume, homemade of course, and meeting with others to run around and act silly. They often went from house to house to play tricks on the older generation; they didn't know anything about trick or treat back in those days.

The old trick of blocking the road was of little excitement, since there were only a few cars—and less traffic—on Coaley Creek.

Teed could not go very far from home on that special night—certainly not as far as Big Onion Gap—to trick people and block roads. So, if he blocked the road, about the only exciting trick that he could pull on someone in the hollow, he blocked the road against his kinfolks in the community. No one in the immediate family owned an automobile, but Uncle Ferd Skinner had a T-Model Ford. It hadn't been moved from its parking place under a toolshed attached to the big log barn for a couple of months. It wasn't likely to be moved that night, either.

The only hope for such excitement would be for someone to come along and stub his toe on the roadblock while walking about the community. Teed could laugh at something like that. He often hoped it would happen, but that hope was to no avail. Even if someone did trip over the barricade, no news of the incident would reach the local newspaper. Actually, no one would hear about it unless someone was seen after Halloween limping around with a sore toe.

For Teed, there was no fun hiding to await a happening like that, since there were few people stirring about and patience was not his forte.

On that special night, Gillis, Satch Hood, and Cousin Jubal had left on a run through the neighborhood in search of some excitement and mischief.

Teed had not decided to go anywhere when the other boys left. That was what he told them. It was rather unusual for Gillis, the other two boys, and Teed to be separated for any reason, other than sleeping, eating, and taking a bath. Well now, maybe they were apart more often than Teed realized.

Teed had heard that a Halloween party was to be held at Big Bull Creek Elementary School, across the mountain from Coaley Creek. That was his planned destination.

Gillis, Satch, and Cousin Jubal dressed up in some gaudy, self-made costumes—the kind in which anyone could recognize them. They wore clothes too large for them and had smeared soot all over their faces. Now, who would not recognize them dressed up like that?

Teed figured that Gillis and his friends would finally end up with Esker and Tester Seedy and really have a great time.

The Seedys would not have to dress up in an odd manner to be ugly. Ugly came easily for them—one of their inheritances.

Teed's costume was simple—his sister's old dress. He wore mascara, lipstick, and a big helping of rouge. A red bandanna covered his head. He combed his hair down over his forehead—almost over his eyes—so that he would look like a girl with bangs. He used some unmentionable articles to give a true female appearance. He really looked nice, especially for a boy dressed like a girl.

With his costume completed, he headed for Big Bull Creek. He had heard that the party included activities for teenagers from the community. Since he had recently become a teenager, he felt that he would fit in well with that crowd on Big Bull Creek. His main objective was to win that prize for best costume. No one could possibly recognize him, he felt. He was too cleverly dressed for that bunch of yokels. Nearly everyone on Big Bull Creek knew Teed, but dressed as he was, they would not know him from a sack of taters. Those people were in for a treat!

Teed intended to win that prize, and that was the main reason for his going alone. He did not need Gillis and those other guys tagging along in the way. The only way to win was to be alone, he reasoned. Their presence could jeopardize his chances of taking that prize by giving away his identity to the crowd, and he wanted that prize of candy, chewing gum, apples, and all kinds of goodies.

The weather was extremely warm for the last of October. Indian summer had set in. That was probably the reason for the high temperature, Teed figured. He wondered why the white folks on Coaley Creek were having an Indian summer without any Indians around to help celebrate it.

As the boy walked along the dusty highway, he feared that he might become too hot and begin to sweat. Perspiration could ruin his mascara by running through it and streaking it all over his face. He was even afraid to sneeze, afraid that his face might crack open and blow off, leaving plain Teed Cornfield.

Time was slowly slipping away, and the teenager had a couple of miles to cover in a hurry.

"Ever'body must be at the party," he thought aloud, looking up the deserted highway.

* * * *

Teed arrived at Big Bull Creek Elementary School just as the sun dropped behind Lick Fork. Darkness flooded the pleasant little valley very quickly. As the boy entered the crowded schoolhouse, Gillis was the first person he saw—that he recognized. He thought for sure that he had left Gillis and those other boys on Coaley Creek where they belonged. He didn't need that bunch around to mess up his plans. When he looked about the dim room, he saw more familiar faces.

Satch Hood, Esker and Tester Seedy, and Cousin Jubal slouched against the wall in the back of the room. And there stood Josie Milt at the front of the room, dressed in a witch's costume, befitting her personality.

One light bulb, hanging down from the center of the ceiling, gave a weak glow about the room. In each corner were deep shadows which would make it easy for Teed to hide, and into their refuge he sneaked.

A huge person, a man Teed did not recognize, stepped on the boy's foot, almost crushing his big toe.

Teed figured that the big man should sit down to get the weight off his feet, but no one was sitting. Maybe the man did not want to be different.

"Pardon me, young lady," the man grunted, apologizing for his awkwardness.

"That's all right, sir. It didn't hurt very much," Teed lied, whispering in a low tone, afraid that he might be recognized as a boy if he were to speak out loud. His voice had begun to change with the arrival of adolescence.

"You should do something about that cold that's left you hoarse," the fat man advised.

"I will," Teed promised, moving away so he wouldn't have to talk to the man. He certainly did not want to stand near someone who wanted to chat, fearing that he might forget to whisper, ruining his chances of winning the prize.

As Teed pulled his mashed toe back away from the end of his shoe, trying to relieve the pain, he noticed that he was still wearing his ankle-high brogan shoes. He had forgotten to change into his sister's brown and white saddle oxfords before leaving home. He would have to tiptoe around to keep from clumping and making a loud noise in his brogans. Well, that might be all right, for tiptoeing would also make him look taller, and just maybe Gillis, that bunch with him, and Josie Milt would fail to recognize him, preserving his chances of winning that prize. Teed looked straight ahead while the little kids were judged for the best costume in the small-kids category. A little boy from Big Bull Creek won the prize of chewing gum, apples, candy, and balloons.

Next in the program was an apple-bobbing contest. It was hard for a kid to grip a big apple in his mouth. Most of those kids were missing their front teeth. There was no way that those little ones could hold on to an apple long enough to lift it above the water to win a prize.

Whenever Teed stole a glance around the room, he saw boys looking at him and whispering among themselves, snickering at something that was said. He tried to get out of sight, but that was impossible.

Esker Seedy winked at Teed and grinned, showing his big tobacco-stained buckteeth.

Teed dropped his head coyly, but not before Esker winked at him again. Boy, Esker Seedy was ugly! Teed couldn't imagine any pretty girl in her right mind responding to his advances in a positive manner. "The joke's on you, my friend," Teed laughed to himself.

If Esker knew that he was flirting with his old buddy Teed Cornfield, he would try to get even with Teed by starting a fight.

Teed wasn't in the mood to fight right then. He wanted to win that prize first. He stayed ready for a good scuffle. Esker could start one anytime he wanted to, after the judging of the costumes, of course. Teed would comply with his wishes, but not until he had possession of that big bag of goodies. He breathed a big sigh of relief when Esker went to the front of the room to bob for apples.

One must admire Esker for his efforts in competing in the game. He was pretty good with those big buckteeth. He could gnaw corn from a cob through a two-inch crack in the wall of a corncrib, if he got hungry enough and wanted to do that.

Esker searched for the largest apple in the three-bushel washing tub. When he found the one that suited his fancy, he tried to grip it with his big buckteeth. He failed on his first try. The apple skipped away from him, but that did not discourage him. A big, ugly smile spread over his face. He tried again. On his second attempt to sink his teeth into the apple, he pushed it to the bottom of the tub with his face. His head disappeared below the rim of the tub, causing the water to flow over the sides, wetting the floor around his knees where he knelt, gripping the rim of the tub with both hands to balance himself.

The crowd roared with laughter as they watched Esker in his efforts to corral the big apple.

After what seemed forever, Esker came up for a lungfull of air, snorting and spluttering to get the water out of his nostrils and mouth. He held the apple firmly between his buckteeth. A broad grin spread far beyond each side of the big fruit. He won an apple of his choice for his efforts. As he returned to the back of the room, he received a roaring round of applause

"That kid surely is an ugly excuse for a human being," Teed thought. Esker walked to the back of the room—toward Teed—and made an offering of the apple that he still held between his dirty teeth. Slobber drooled from the corners of his ugly mouth.

"Here's a big apple for you, cutie," he said, taking the apple in his dirty hand and offering it to Teed, still smiling in his friendly way. "I would give you this prize apple, but it's too small for a prize like you." He held the bit-on apple out for Teed to accept.

"No thanks," Teed whispered, trying desperately to disguise his voice so he would not be recognized.

"Take it, cutie," Esker encouraged, trying in an honest, good-natured way to coax his friend to accept the apple. When he was unable to persuade Teed to take it, he looked for a pocket to put it in, and finding no pockets on the dress, he left it lying on the desk next to Teed. "You can eat it as I walk you home, and I can eat this 'un," Esker said, trying to make a date with the pretty girl.

"Sweet-talk that pretty girl," Satch Hood said, joining the other boys laughing at their friend's efforts to get the attention of the attractive stranger.

"I'm spreading on the 'lasses. I think I'm doing pretty good, too. I've got her wropped around my little finger," Esker bragged, speaking loud enough for everyone in the crowded room to hear him.

"Boy, is there a surprise in store for you!" Teed mumbled.

Esker continued to make goo-goo eyes at Teed each time Teed looked in the direction of his ugly friend. And that bunch of silly boys with Esker laughed at his attempts to woo the stranger.

Finally, the time came for the judging of the teenager's costumes. A man and a woman went among the crowd, looking at the different costumes, picking out the most unique.

"You can go to the front of the room," the man told a little boy dressed as a cowboy, sporting a red bandanna over his mouth and nose. "You can go up front, too," he said, stopping in front of a girl dressed as a witch.

Several more children were selected before the woman came to Teed.

Teed held his breath, afraid to breathe. He was afraid that he might give away his identity by just breathing.

"Go the front of the room, young lady," the woman summoned, smiling pleasantly at Teed.

Teed walked up the aisle to take his place in the line of boys and girls, tiptoeing along as daintily as he could to keep from clumping. He heard the man tell Tester Seedy to go to the front of the room.

"All right!" Tester yelled, running up the aisle. He caught up with Teed, tiptoeing along to keep from clomping too loudly, afraid that the clomping might draw attention and reveal his real identity.

Tester swatted Teed on the bottom with his open hand, speeding the imposter along, bringing a roar of laughter from the amused crowd.

Tester was trying to flirt with Teed but chose the wrong approach. As he stood beside Teed at the front of the room, along with the rest of the contestants, a big smile splitting his uncomely face, he reached down and slyly took Teed's hand. That brought a surprised look to his face. He jerked his hand free. "This ain't no girl! It's...."

The surprised boy's statement ended as he received a punch in the mouth.

Teed smiled as Tester landed on his back on the floor. He rubbed his cut knuckles, caused by the impact of his fist against Tester's dirty teeth.

The teacher restored order and reprimanded Tester for attempting to disclose a contestant's identity.

Teed feared that he might have to leave the room, that is if someone could identify him and take away his chance to win the prize.

"You sure have dry, rusty hands for a pretty girl. And just look at that humongous, crooked nose sticking out of your face like a warped stick of baloney," Tester bantered, continuing to give hints to the four boys at the back of the room.

"That's enough, young man," Mr. Tedder, the teacher, warned. "I will have to send you to your seat and not let you participate in this contest. And I will if you give any more trouble. Now let's commence our judging. If anyone in the audience can recognize a contestant, that contestant loses his chance to participate further and will have to sit down."

"I know who that red-faced girl up there is!" Esker Seedy shouted, air whistling through his tobacco-stained buckteeth.

"Yeah," Satch Hood echoed. "No girl could floor ol' Tester like that. There's only one person I know that can punch that hard, and it sure ain't a girl!"

"Yeah, and I know who owns them shoes with the creeled-over heels." Gillis laughed. "I'd know that pair of shoes anywhere I met them."

"Quiet! Quiet!" Mr. Tedder ordered. "Wait until we get to a person before you attempt to identify her, or him, or whichever it might be."

Order was restored and the judging of the costumes began. The first contestant was Josie Milt. She was easily recognized by Tester Seedy and his friends.

"That's ol' Josie Milt from over on Coaley Creek!" the boys yelled.

Josie Milt left the line of contestants, stamping her feet to show her frustrations. She could never lose gracefully.

Teed would hate to lose, and as he became more dubious of his chances of remaining anonymous, the anxiety became almost intolerable. He felt that he stood a good chance of winning, but he couldn't be sure. Those boys in the back of the room were only trying to guess his identity. They really didn't know who he was, he hoped.

Finally, Teed was next in line to be identified. Could that bunch really guess who he was? He stood there with his hands behind his back, his fingers crossed, hoping that no one would be lucky enough to recognize him.

"Now, my friends," Mr. Tedder said, smiling at Teed, "who is this young lady?

"Teed Cornfield!" came from the mouths of four boys in the back of the room. Tears streamed down their cheeks as they laughed uproariously.

"Teed would be a right pretty girl if he wore girl's shoes," Esker Seedy laughed.

"Yeah, his shoes sure don't go with that dress," Gillis chimed. "And we know who Tester Seedy is. Come and sit down, Tester."

Tester went to the back of the room, giving Teed a wide berth as he left the remaining contestants, who were waiting to be recognized.

Teed remained in line. He wasn't going to give up that easily. It was just possible that each contestant would be recognized, and then the judges might have to divide the prize between someone else and Teed, since his costume was so good that he had boys flirting with him, thinking he was a girl. He surely had everyone fooled! If it had not been for that hateful Tester Seedy giving away his identity, Teed figured that he could have won the prize, hands down. He would settle with that boy later on in the evening.

The last person to be identified was the little fellow dressed as a cowboy with the bandanna over his face. No one could guess who he was.

When the bandanna was finally removed, there stood the shyest, prettiest little girl that Teed had ever seen in his entire life. My, but she was beautiful! She had long black hair that tumbled down her back when she removed her hat. She had a pretty little mouth and a turned-up nose.

"My daughter, Doe Tedder, folks," the teacher said, bowing to the crowd.

After the raucous round of applause ceased, the room became very quiet once more.

Teed was glad that Doe Tedder had won. If he had won that prize, the way he felt right then, he would have given her that big bag of goodies. He wanted to talk to her, but how could he get up enough courage to try? There he stood, wearing a dress, makeup, and a pair of creeled-over shoes.

There was another round of applause for all the contestants, causing the schoolhouse to resound with the clapping of many hands.

When Teed turned his attentions back to the little girl, there was Gillis, talking to her and eating the goodies that she had given him.

Teed had lost both—the goodies and the girl—due to his goofy brother and his corny friends from Coaley Creek.

Koodank Goes Airborne

Teed and Gillis laid two long poles, about six inches in diameter, across the little stream that meandered through the swampy area of the little hillside farm. One pole was secured in the bed of the creek, while the other stretched from bank to bank. There were numerous seams of coal at different levels beneath the steep slopes that reached toward the sky. Springs of mineral-filled water came to the surface at those coal seams and flowed into the valley between the hills, forming the stream of slow-moving water. In a few places the creek was about ten feet wide and ten inches deep. At one of the deep spots, the boys decided to build a swimming hole.

The boys built their form for the dam by nailing short boards to the two poles laid across the stream. They daubed the cracks between the boards with clay mud from the edge of the creek. Over the clay caulking they placed pieces of sod cut from the swampy meadow near the stream. The roots of the grass held the clay soil in their grasp, creating a good material for a strong dam.

The water was contained fairly well, with only minor leaks. If a storm should happen to blow in, the extra water pressure would cause the stream to fill its banks and run with enough force to push the little dam downstream. If that should happen, the boys would build another dam to replace the one demolished by the storm. It had happened before and could happen again, Teed and Gillis realized.

The boys were like two beavers, working hard, not giving up in their quest to build a long-lasting swimming hole.

The dam was finished, and the fantastic swimming hole was ready to catch enough water for the boys to begin dabbling and taking a good mud bath, as they called their swimming sessions.

Their thrashing around in the water stirred up the sediment on the bottom of the stream. The muddy mess was composed of gravels, half-rotted leaves, and insects and their larvae. One larva was a leech. They did not know whether or not it was a true leech, but that was what they called it. They had been told that those little larvae were leeches. They were also told that if one should happen to bite them, it wouldn't let go—might even eat its way into their bodies. They beat several bits of leaves to a pulp, thinking they were the dreaded leeches clinging to their bodies. The boys were scared of those little suckers. Even though they had never had one on their bodies, they were afraid of the mere thought of an attack by one and were ever on the alert to avoid them.

Their parents had often told them that if a leech should get a tooth sunk in, it would hold on until it thundered. The lads did not know whether or not that was true, but they knew for a certainty that turtles would hold on that way, so leeches could, too. They did not want to take any unnecessary, stupid chances, so they checked each other often for the dreaded leeches.

The weather had been extremely dry that summer—very few thunderstorms. The boys would have been in big trouble had a leech attached itself to a leg and they had had to wait for thunder to make it turn loose.

Teed and Gillis were having a great time, although they were kept busy trying to keep the mud out of their eyes.

Gillis looked at Teed with his irritated eyes snapping and blinking. He tried to clear out the muddy water that had entered them when he did one of the greatest belly-buster dives ever attempted by man.

"Gillis," Teed laughed, "your eyes look like two slices of 'matoes laying out in the yard in a snowbank. I never saw such red eyes before in my whole life."

"Yours are just as red as mine, Teed, and I don't care," Gillis said, gripping his nose between an index finger and thumb. He sank below the surface of the muddy water once more, causing bubbles of air to come to the surface and pop like popcorn in a skillet.

Teed laughed and dived in after Gillis. He groped about in the murky stream, searching for his brother.

Koodank arrived on the scene just as the bigger boys came to the surface and staggered about, trying to find a secure footing on the soft bottom of the stream.

"Why are you snooping around here, Koodank?" Gillis asked, wiping his eyes with a pair of dirty hands.

"Mom said for you boys to come and help pick some beans," he said, taking a seat on a rock at the edge of the swimming hole to watch his brothers splash about in the water. "Why can't I swim with you big boys?" he asked.

"'Cause you're just a little snot-nose is why you can't get in here with us big guys," Gillis replied, diving into the pond once more. He thrashed and kicked around, imitating a swimmer.

"I'm just as big as you are, Gillis," Koodank whined. He sat all hunched over on a rock at the edge of the swimming hole, disappointed, wanting to swim with the big boys.

"Why didn't you tell Mom that we went away, maybe to join the Army?" Gillis said, splashing around, then diving into the water. When he rose to the surface, his hair was filled with guck, causing it to cling to his forehead. He spluttered the water out of his mouth and wiped his eyes with the backs of his hands in an effort to dislodge the mud. "Go tell Mom that you couldn't find us," he said after he had cleared the mud out of his eyes and the water from his lungs by coughing and spitting into the swimming hole. "Tell her that we got picked up by some folks from outer space. Now we're up there saucerin' around in the universe, checking out the stars and planets and comets and asteroids and meteorites and playing with a couple of pretty little Martian girls with cotton wads for eyeballs."

"I would be lying and get a good whuppin' if I did that," Koodank said. "I'll go tell Mom that you'll be right there."

Koodank was a very honest kid. Teed had never known him to lie— not even once. He admired the kid for his honesty and truthfulness, but right then he could have choked him. Teed wanted to swim, but no, "Honest Abe" Koodank had to go and ruin everything by finding him. Teed would have to pick the beans sooner or later, he realized, but he did not want to do it right at that very moment. He wanted to swim. Swimming was much more fun than picking beans any old time.

"Koodank, you little runt, why don't you go hide and stay there for awhile? Then go tell Mom that you can't find us," Teed suggested.

"Mom knows where you're at," Koodank replied. "We could hear your racket from way over there at the house. You can't fool Mom, Teed."

"I'm not trying to fool Mom," Teed came back. "Can't you see that I'm not here? This place is deserted and quiet. No one is around here. Deserted."

"No you're not hid from me, Teed," Koodank declared. "Do you think that I'm blind? I have two good eyes and one good nose."

"What does a nose have to do with finding us?" Gillis wondered. "You can't smell us."

"Yes I can smell you boys," Koodank replied. "You smell like a frog pond. You've stirred up a big mud stink."

Gillis and Teed couldn't smell Koodank sitting all humped up on that big rock. How could the kid smell them?

"You boys had better get a move on and help pick them beans. If Daddy comes home from work early, you'll be in a peck of trouble." Koodank said, then jumped off the rock and ran toward the house.

"I'll get you for this, you little smart aleck," Teed called to the wind. Koodank was out of sight and out of hearing. "The little runt's allus messing up a good time. His day is coming, though. I'll get even with him if it's the last thing I do," he grumbled.

"Oh, just forget Koodank, Teed," Gillis said. "He's only doing what Mom told him to do. Come on. Let's get that patch of beans under control. I hate beans now, but they'll be mighty tasty when wintertime comes. They'll be a whole lot better than a snowball on your plate."

"That ain't much consolation right now," Teed grumbled, trying to wipe the mud, grass, and leaves from his legs. "Why can't we raise things that don't have to be picked, strung, broke, cut, hoed, pulled, weeded, and harvested? Why do children have to work, anyway? If we didn't have to work all the time, we could just play and make swimming holes all summer long. Then in the wintertime we could make sleds and ride them in the snow. Farm boys have a rough, hard life, if you ask me. Tut Duddle lives in town.

He says that he don't have to do anything that keeps him from going swimming, riding his bike, or going to the movies. He told me that he does all them things ever' day—weekends, too. Now, wouldn't that be a good life? I tell you for a fact that farm boys sure have it rough."

"Let's go get started on that bunch of beans, Teed. The sooner we get started, you know, the sooner we'll finish," Gillis said, finishing dressing.

The rows of beans stretched for miles it seemed. Teed didn't know whether the mile had been shortened a little or the rows had been lengthened a lot. There was one thing for sure, though: they had enough beans in that field for everyone on Coaley Creek.

The sun was torturous, and Teed's grumbling did not help matters any. He had a job to do, and showing his contrariness and discomforts would not help to speed up the work. He thought that he needed some form of entertainment, so he suggested a word game or any interesting challenge to offset the misery of work. He needed some competitive pleasure, if one could have pleasure in a bean field. Only one living creature can have pleasure in a bean patch—a bean beetle.

"Gillis, let's give out initials of people we know or have heard of," Teed suggested.

"That's all right with me. How does that sound to you girls?" Gillis asked his sisters.

"That's fine with us," Skatney and Friday said, agreeing with the proposal.

"I'll play, too," Koodank offered. "I think I'll go first."

"I'll go first," Teed told his little brother. "T. K. Does anyone know what that stands for? If you don't, it stands for 'Thumped Koodank,' and that's what you're going to be, Mister Smarty, if you don't get out of the way," Teed threatened.

Koodank whimpered as he walked out toward his mother at the opposite end of the bean patch, his little body heaving and retching in a disappointed cry.

"Now, gang, since the main source of our aggravation is gone out of our hair, we can get on with the game," Teed said, grinning like a skinned squirrel. "Now," he continued, "let's give out the initials of cowboys, country singers, presidents, congressmen, senators, governors, uncles, aunts, cousins, brothers, sisters, sheriffs, friends, acquaintances, cats, dogs, chickens, goats, or anything that you can think of."

"All right, but don't you think you were just a little rough on Koodank? Leave him alone," Skatney said, a touch of anger rising in her voice. "Koodank is little and ain't bothering you. I might do some thumping of my own if you keep up harassin' him all the time."

"You and who else, big girl?" Teed asked, showing his courage, even though he knew very well that Skatney could punch, wrestle, bite, and pull hair as well as any boy. He gave her plenty of walking space, but he could not afford to let her know that he dreaded a confrontation with her. More than once she had given him reason to have a little fear of her.

"I'll show you just how many it will take to put you in your place," Skatney said, throwing her bean pail on the ground and approaching Teed with the intent of giving him a thrashing.

While all that action was taking place, Koodank told his mother that Teed was picking on him.

"Whip Teed, Mom," Koodank pleaded, snubbing and wiping his nose and eyes with the heels of his hands.

"What are you big young 'uns doing to Koodank?" Vann asked as Skatney neared Teed's bean row, where Teed had planted his feet in a good position to land the first blow, and he was sure that it would have been his only blow, because Skatney had that look of annihilation in her sparkling brown eyes.

Skatney stopped short of giving Teed the thumping of his life.

Teed was glad that his mother intervened right at that moment. His courage began to rise to the surface once more. It had dropped to his toes and would have gone farther had he not been wearing his shoes. "We ain't doing anything to him," he said. "He just wants to cause me a lot of trouble."

"He doesn't have to cause your troubles, Teed. You stay in trouble all the time," Vann told him.

"Yes, he's in big trouble with me," Skatney said, loud enough for Vann to hear.

"Skatney, you and Teed are too big to be arguing with each other like that," Vann said, returning to the chore of picking beans. "You kids get back to work. I won't tell you again."

Vann Cornfield was a very easygoing person, but at that moment she sounded like someone on the verge of losing her temper. The children knew that she would take care of matters if she happened to get riled up just right.

"I'm just as big as Skatney, and just as tough, too," Teed boasted. "Just let her try to brawl with me. Then she'll see what a wildcat I am."

"If you don't get back to picking beans, I know a wildcat that's going to get skinned," Vann threatened, and Teed could see that she was serious. "Now, if you're as big as Skatney, act like it." She rose from her crouched position, an indication that she meant what she said.

As Skatney laughed in that humiliating way, which she often did so deliberately, Teed became more irate. "Your day's coming, Skatney," he threatened, keeping his voice too low for his mother to hear that he and his sister were still bickering.

"Teed, you'll get a whipping before this day's over. If not from me, then from Dad or Mom," Skatney prophesied.

"It certainly won't be from a little ol' taggy girl like you, Skatney!" Teed stormed, looking at her with a churlish sneer. "I'm just as tough as they make boys these days, and real hard to hit."

"No, you won't be the one that gets to put the whup-ups on him, Skatney, 'cause you won't be able to catch him," Gillis said, laughing at the thought of Skatney having to catch Teed in order to give him a shellacking.

The arguing and bickering continued among the kids while they worked, but in a tone so low that their mother could not hear them. The arguments made the time pass faster, and finally the bean-picking chore was finished.

Reluctantly, Teed started the much-dreaded chore of preparing the beans for canning. He was still mad and upset with Koodank and Skatney.

Every move they made rubbed him the wrong way.

Little Koodank tried to help with stringing the beans for canning. He was too small to be of any help at all. He broke the beans without first stringing them. He threw bug-bit pieces in with the clean beans.

"Koodank, why don't you get out of the way and let us finish this pile of beans?" Teed suggested. "If you keep throwing in scrap pieces, we'll never finish. Why don't you go play somewhere? Go ride your tricycle. Do something that will keep you busy and out of the way. Ride your tricycle around the porch with your eyes closed. That will keep you busy for a while. See if you can ride all the way around the porch. You're a good rider. You can pretend that it's a racetrack and conquer the course."

"That will be easy for a good rider like me," the little fellow bragged, running to get his tricycle from its usual place in the corner near the kitchen door.

The porch ran the entire length of the big farmhouse—maybe forty feet in length—then made a ninety-degree turn and extended another twenty feet. It was about eight feet wide.

Koodank mounted the tricycle and peddled it across the porch with his eyes closed. He was able to maneuver part of the course all right. He did well on the straight part but was unable to make the quick turn to his left. With his eyes closed tightly, he had no sense of direction, and over the edge of the porch he went—airborne—landing in a bunch of kudzu vines.

The vines ran from the ground all the way to the eaves, held up by heavy strings. Vann kept them as a decorative plant. They also created a cool, refreshing shade that helped make the afternoon heat more bearable.

Koodank screamed like a cat stepped on as he lay in a crumpled heap at the base of the porch. The five-foot fall had been cushioned by the bulk of the kudzu vines. He wasn't really hurt, but the suddenness of the fall into space as he went airborne had more of an effect on him than the pain. Anyway, he was doing a good job of expressing his discomforts by crying.

Everyone ran to his rescue—all except Teed. "He'll live. Just don't make such a fuss over him," he said as Vann, Skatney, Gillis, and Friday peered down at the pathetic little fellow.

"That wasn't such a big deal," Teed thought. "That little fall—anyone could fall that well. There's no reason to get all out of kilter and go heel over hoe handle because of such a little calamity."

The situation was amusing to Teed. He laughed. He was getting even with Koodank for his finding him at the good swimming hole. His brother was the cause of Teed's having to pick beans. He figured that the water was probably running over the dam right about then, and there he was, hobbled by a bean pile. He wanted to go swimming, while his brother, sisters, and mother were making such a fuss over Koodank's fall.

Teed rose from his seat and attempted to sneak away to the swimming hole. He froze in that awkward position when he heard his father's strong voice.

"What happened to little Koodank down there all balled up in them vines with his tricycle? Are you stuck, Son?" Marn asked as he joined the rest of the family looking down at the little boy.

Everyone stood and looked without making an effort to free Koodank from those monster vines holding him captive.

Teed looked at Koodank for the first time, since he was already up. He saw that the little fellow's legs were all wrapped around the handlebars of the tricycle. His head was stuck in the vines, and the front wheel was on his right hand. That would teach the kid to leave the big boys alone the next time they went swimming.

"He's not stuck," Vann said, elucidating Koodank's plight. "He tried to ride his tricycle with his eyes closed and went sailing into space."

"Teed told me to," Koodank wailed as his father helped him unwind from his crumpled-up position in the vines. He continued to cry and snub.

"Did you tell him to ride his tricycle off the porch?" Marn asked, turning to Teed.

"No! I did not!" Teed retorted. "He was in our way here while we were stringing these beans. I told him to go play and get out of the way so we could work. I just suggested that he try to ride his tricycle with his eyes closed, but I didn't think that he would be stupid enough to ride it over the edge of the porch like that."

"Teed, you know that Koodank's too little to know when you boys are joshing him," Marn said. "You know that he respects you boys and looks up to you. He'll do just about anything that you older boys tell him to do."

"I didn't tell him to do it. I told him to ride around there to have fun while we did our work," Teed replied. "He needed a challenge and he was right in the way."

"Well, Teed, we'll see who's right in the way," Marn threatened, then went to cut a switch.

Teed tried to get even with his little brother, but instead, the little brother got even with Teed.

Bat Rock

The older children had grown up and moved away from Coaley Creek. There were four children left at home—Teed, Gillis, Friday, and Koodank. The big nest was almost empty, leaving Teed as the oldest child at home. Since he was a teenager, he found himself the leader of the gang. He had become a cutup and a comic, always pulling pranks on the younger siblings, teasing and aggravating them. He would do anything for a laugh.

On any given day the children were constantly playing or working—never idle—always doing something.

Teed and Gillis were boxing with their new stuffed-sock gloves, giving each other a few good jabs, left hooks, and right crosses. Teed expected Gillis to kick his shins at any moment. Each time they sparred a little, Gillis usually ended the bout with a well-placed kick to one of Teed's unprotected shins.

Gillis was small and fast—good with a left jab, drop to a left hook to Teed's right side—low often—then a right cross. Usually the low left hook did more damage than the rest of his arsenal. He surely was a fast little scutter—hard to hit.

Teed had a pretty good arsenal, too. He had learned quickly that he could put up a much better defense with his face than he could with both of his fists.

Gillis was a good fleaweight, probably the lightest weight of all. Surely he would grow a lot more. Maybe one day he would be a gnatweight. Only time would tell.

Teed had just received a hard shot to the chin when he heard his mother calling. When Gillis dropped his guard to listen, Teed took advantage of the opportunity, catching Gillis with a pretty good left hook on the back of his shoulder as he turned away. What a surprise! Teed didn't know whether he was getting a little better or if Gillis was slipping a lot. Anyway, that one good punch was a good ego booster for Teed.

"Hey, Teed, Gillis, and Arr! Where are you boys?" Vann yelled. She had to yell. The boys could not hear her when she called to them in a normal tone. Most of the time they were usually too far away or making too much of a racket to hear their mother calling to them. And, too, they often turned a deaf ear to any summons from their mother. But when Marn yelled, the kids put it in high gear to heed his beck and call.

Usually the boys were far away from the house, at the farthest corner of their favorite arena of action, inside a ring made by an imaginary line that circled the entire forty acres—more or less—of the farm.

Teed had actually punched Gillis with one of his lucky left hooks, and the little brother, forgetting that he was boxing at the moment, prepared to get even by aiming a right foot at his opponent's left shin.

The least little thing could get Gillis riled, causing him to forget about boxing, turning him to the art of country fighting. Using anything for defense or offense is country fighting, and Gillis often used everything when he got mad—a one hundred percent country fighter. Gillis stopped in mid-kick when he heard Vann calling again.

"Did you hear anything, Gillis?" Teed asked, cupping his gloved hand behind his ear to be able to hear better. He had often seen his grandfather, Dalker Skinner, do that when someone spoke to him.

"No, I didn't hear Mom yell at all," Gillis replied. He listened for another call from Vann.

"Friday, have you seen Teed, Gillis, and Arr?" Vann asked the little girl, who was playing with a rag doll, running about the front porch with the doll held tightly against her cheek, singing lullabies to it.

Arr was riding his tricycle on the walk which ran from the house to the well at the edge of the yard—a good place for the little fellow to ride safely.

"Arr is right here with me, Mom," Friday replied. "I heard Teed and Gillis out behind the smokehouse or somewhere, scuffling, snorting, and grunting around. They're boxing again. Maybe if they beat each other up, they might quit that foolish stuff. Seems like that's all that they want to do anymore—just beat, punch, grunt, snort, and whine around. Looks to me like that they could do something else for their excitement, don't you, Mom?"

"Aw, beating on each other is fun to them, looks like. They're having fun. They're trying to prove to us that they're tough. Go tell them that I need some dry stove wood so I can cook your supper," she ordered. "Tell them," she continued her directive, "that I need some kindling wood, too, so I can get a fire started."

"All right, Mom," Friday answered, and obediently began her search for the boys. She knew where to look for them and went straight to the two combatants.

The boys remained as silent as two fence posts. Having fun was much better than work, especially if that work was chopping wood. Boxing was more fun than chopping wood any old time.

Friday found Teed and Gillis and called out to Arr, who continued to ride his tricycle on the walk. "Here they are, Arr. They're whuppin' up on each other."

"Now we can watch them put the whup-ups on a log while they make wood for Mom," Koodank laughed, squeaking like a baby chipmunk.

"I'll beat up on you, Koodank," Gillis threatened, chasing the little fellow away, his homemade boxing gloves at the ready to pounce on him.

It was only a threat. It is very doubtful that he would have hurt the lad on purpose.

Teed would have intervened had Gillis tried to rough up Koodank.

Koodank was a fine kid, but the big boys got a little peeved with him at times. They ignored him as they hung the boxing gloves on two nails in the smokehouse wall and went to commence their chore.

"Get the crosscut saw, Gillis," Teed ordered. "And you, Koodank," he further demanded, "get out of my hair and sit on those steps and watch. He pointed to a set of fieldstone steps that provided access from the lower level of the woodyard to the lawn.

Obediently, Koodank sat on the steps. He looked so disappointed sitting there so small—about as big as handful of nothing.

Teed regretted speaking to the tyke with such a curt tone, but he had to in order to keep the little brother in line. If he let Koodank get by with laughing at them, the little fellow would think that he could get by with anything he wished. Teed couldn't let that happen. Yes, Teed could do a thing like that, he figured. He was much bigger, and he had the right to rat on others and play pranks on them. Since Koodank was so little, the kid had no such privileges. That was the way Teed looked at the situation. He was the tattler and the prankster in the family, and as far as he was concerned, it would have to stay that way.

Gillis returned from the coalhouse, where he had taken the crosscut saw from its place on the wall. A two-nail rack—two twenty-penny nails driven into the two-by-fours supporting the walls of the building—was the resting place for the saw during its idle moments. The workshop was about one hundred yards from the house, while the coalhouse was a mere twenty yards away. Keeping the saw at the coalhouse saved the boys a lot of walking each day.

"Gillis, help me roll this log over on that other one," Teed said, pointing to the two logs that were to be used for firewood.

The logs were wormy chestnut about twelve inches in diameter at the butt. Chestnut wood, a good source of fuel for cooking a quick meal in a wood-burning range, gives off a quick, intense heat.

The boys needed to roll one of the logs across the other in order to hold it above the rock-filled earth to prevent the saw from striking the rocks beneath the log. Sawing wood with a sharp saw is a hard task. The chore is much harder when one is stuck with a dull tool. Marn had taught his boys well in taking care of the tools.

Finally, with much effort, with Teed using a cant hook, and Gillis using a sourwood pole as a lever, they managed to roll one of the logs on top of the other. The top log would have to be made secure so it would not roll when they attempted to cut it into the correct lengths to fit the firebox of their mother's stove.

Gillis secured his side of the log with a double-bitted axe by striking both logs with the axe blade. One side cut into the bottom log while the other side cut into the top log, holding it in place.

It was Teed's turn to make fast his side of the log. He lifted his axe as far above his head as he could before swinging it downward with all his strength. His aim was off just a little. The handle struck the top of the log at such an angle that it went out of control. The handle bounced up and struck Teed under the chin, jarring him from his teeth to his toes, causing stars to flash before his eyes.

Teed had his mouth open as he said, "Hah!" to drive the axe deep into the log. His mouth was open at the time the axe met the logs, but it did not stay open very long. His jaws plopped together with a resounding snap, causing his teeth to meet with so much force that small pieces of enamel flew out of his mouth. It hurt a lot worse than he wanted to admit. He grabbed his injured chin with both hands and humped and gimped around in pain. When he looked around the woodyard, Gillis was bent over, laughing so hard that he could hardly stand up, and there sat Koodank on the steps, squeak-laughing with his mouth wide-open.

At first glance, Teed thought that Koodank resembled a little chipmunk, but when he looked at him again, he thought differently. Koodank was at that tooth-shedding age and had lost four of his front teeth.

Teed was mad at Gillis and Koodank for laughing at him, but when he looked at toothless Koodank, he had to chuckle. The kid looked so comical, sitting there like a little knot on a stump.

"Why do such things have a different outlook when they happen to me instead of someone else?" Teed mumbled. If that mishap had befallen Gillis, it would have been funny, but since it had happened to Teed, he did not think it was such an entertaining incident.

Teed had to vent his frustrations toward someone, and that someone would have to be Koodank, since the kid could not protect himself against such a big person like Teed. "Get out of my sight and stop your silly chipmunk-squeak laughing," he demanded, making a threatening gesture by running toward his little brother in an effort to scare him away.

Koodank ran up the steps and headed toward the protection of the house and his mother. "Boy, there was enough teeth flew out of your mouth to feed the chickens for a whole week!" he yelled over his shoulder as he continued his mad dash for the house.

"You'll think chicken feed when I get my hands on you, little boy. I'll get even with you for that!" Teed threatened.

Koodank heard nothing. He was already inside the house.

Teed returned to his efforts to secure the log with the axe. He did much better on the second try, and soon the boys were ready to commence sawing the wood. They proceeded to make firewood as they cut the log into small blocks.

Gillis was amused with Teed's sudden encounter with the axe handle. A smile had taken up residence on his mouth, and it looked like it was there to stay. Gillis was making good use of its presence. He was the type of person who would always take advantage of anything that was free. He was using that free smile to the limit.

Teed looked toward Gillis' end of the saw often. Each time he glanced in that direction, he saw his tickled brother enjoying a silent laugh.

The brothers finished their wood-cutting chore without further mishap.

Later on that evening, Vann had a sumptuous supper as usual.

After that good meal was over, Teed invited Koodank to go with him to look at some minnows in the stream that meandered its way past the corn-crib.

Koodank was so little and gullible that he had no idea his big brother was planning to get even with him for laughing so hard at the chin-smacking incident.

Bats flew about as the day waned into evening. The sun had set and night was fast approaching. The flying mammals dipped down and then rose back up as they caught the night insects that had begun to emerge from their secret hiding places after a long day of rest.

"Look at them bats up there, Koodank," Teed said, pointing out the little animals as they flew helter-skelter above the crib in their efforts to curb their ravenous appetites. "Brother, did you know that a bat will sense a moving rock and follow it if you toss the rock straight up into the air in front of it? Watch this." He tossed a rock about the size of a hen egg into the air as a bat flew over, about twenty feet above the boys' heads.

The bat zeroed in on the rock immediately and followed it, head-first, toward the ground. It did not follow it all the way down. After sensing that it had been tricked, the bat changed its course and flew back to a higher altitude, where it continued to search for a meal of its favorite insects.

"Now, what do you think of that, little brother?" Teed asked.

"That's something else, ain't it, Teed?" Koodank said, amazed by the bat's actions toward the moving stone.

"Do you want to see that again, Koodank?" Teed asked, searching in the semi-darkness for another stone.

"Yeah, try it again, Brud," Koodank said, jumping around excitedly.

Teed tossed another small rock into the air, and once more a bat followed it toward the ground, dropping below the silhouette of the corn-crib, completely out of sight of the two boys.

"Where did it go, Teed?" Koodank asked, straining his eyes, searching for the bat in the darkness.

"I don't know. It might've chased that rock all the way to the ground and busted its head on a rock. Let's look for it," Teed suggested.

"Not me!" Koodank exclaimed, remaining as close to the ground as he could without lying prone upon the grass-covered creek bank.

Teed pretended to search for the fallen bat. Actually, he was feeling around in the dark for another small rock. He found one and picked it up. He walked over to where Koodank squatted, waiting for Teed to find the bat.

Koodank could not see his big brother. The evening had grown completely dark. It was then too dark for a person to see two feet in front of his face.

"I suppose we'd better go to the house, Koodank," Teed said, moving aimlessly around the little creek, pretending to search for the bat.

"Did you find it?" Koodank asked, curiosity getting the best of him. He rose from his crouched position by the stream.

"I sure did," Teed told him.

"Where is it?" Koodank wanted to know, his curiosity rising further, almost to the bursting point. "I'd like to see what a bat looks like up close in person, eyeball to eyeball," he said, moving a little closer in order to inspect the downed bat. "Where is it? I can't see it. It's got too dark to see anything."

"Right here it is," Teed told him, dropping the rock into the little boy's back pocket.

Koodank screamed like a cat with its tail caught in a sausage grinder. He then ran toward the house, yelling for his father.

Teed did his best to catch the kid and remove the rock from his pocket, but to no avail. The little fellow was so scared and ran so fast that Teed was unable to even get close to catching him. He could not understand how Koodank ran among all those rocks without stubbing a toe and falling flat on his face.

The light from the living room outlined Marn as he came through the open door onto the porch.

"What's wrong, Koodank?" Marn asked as the little fellow continued to run and squall.

"Teed put a bat in my pocket!" he screamed, loud enough to burst his lungs.

"Teed, come here right now!" Marn ordered.

Teed knew what that tone of voice meant. Another little prank had backfired on him.

Friday Gets a Charge

Teed lived on Coaley Creek the first thirteen years of his life. He was excited beyond explanation when he learned that he would be moving away from his old home. He looked forward to living on Blue Domer Creek, where he would be able to continue his education. He was eager to enroll in the new school, to begin studying, doing homework, preparing for a future.

Moving from one locality to another is a monumental undertaking in that it throws everything out of kilter. Everyone has to adapt to a new environment, start a new life, and accept new friends and neighbors. Even though some new neighbors cannot be accepted, one has to live with the situation and make the most of any predicament which he is thrown into when moving to a new locale.

The Cornfields had no insurmountable problems when they moved from Coaley Creek to Blue Domer Creek, a distance of about fifteen miles as the crow flies, but twenty *long* miles by the highway.

A large coal company came to Coaley Creek to core-drill in search of coal. The company knew that the fossil fuel was present in the area, but what wasn't known was the size and number of seams lying undisturbed beneath the silent earth. They, the officials of the company, wanted to core-drill to see if it would be feasible to invest in a mining venture there. Evidently there was sufficient evidence found by core-drilling to make such an endeavor worthwhile. The coal company bought the Cornfields' farm, along with all the other farms on Coaley Creek.

The Cornfield children couldn't understand why a coal company would want to search from something of value in the ground on their farm. They had dug all over the place, searching for treasure—something of real value—and had found nothing to pay them for their many hours of labor. Maybe they had given up too quickly—didn't dig deep enough.

Marn and Vann told the children that they had received a fair sum of money for the farm, and with that money they purchased a farm of seventy-two acres, more or less, and who knows which, because they never had it surveyed. That was what the deed called for, and there were no questions about the validity of the paper. Marn and Vann Cornfield were trusting people and trusted the people from whom they purchased their new farm.

During the summer, after the purchase of the new farm, repairs had to be made to the farm buildings. The barn needed a new roof, and the corncrib needed a new roof and a new floor. A chicken pen and a roosting area for the poultry flock had to be built. Fences were mended and new wire strung for new fences to contain the horses and cows. The old fences were broken and in poor condition. The previous owners of the farm had had no real need for fences. They had no livestock to confine.

Teed and Gillis enjoyed going to Blue Domer Creek to work on the farm buildings. Their father took them to a little country store, about a mile down the road, to buy lunches of potted meat and crackers. They even had pop with their meals. Marn often bought sardines and crackers for his lunch.

"You know," Judge L. said one day while he and the boys sat under the barn-shed eating their lunches, "potted meat has to be the best food that was ever invented. It must be the food of the gods." He smacked his lips to indicate that he enjoyed eating potted meat and wiped his mouth, using the back of his hand as a napkin. "This is the best food that I have ever sunk a tooth in."

No one disagreed with him.

*   *   *   *

The warm summer days passed and turned into early fall. The farm buildings had been repaired and the fences mended. The early harvested crops had been moved to Blue Domer Creek. The hay and oats were safe and dry in the barn. Several extra stacks of hay and corn fodder filled a fenced lot nearby.

All that was left to move on that memorable October 16, 1949, was the house plunder, as Marn and Vann called the furniture and other things of necessity. That was the day Teed left Coaley Creek for good.

Bart drove Marn's new 1949 Chevrolet pickup truck, and Teed's uncle, Sprocket Cornfield, drove a huge coal-hauling truck to move the heavy items such as the coal-burning cookstove, tables and chairs, and bedroom furniture.

Uncle Sprocket, his son Boots, and Judge L. rode in the big coal-hauling truck. Cousin Boots came along with his father to help with the moving, or maybe he just came along to get away for home for the day. Anyway, he was in the truck with Uncle Sprocket and Judge L.

Bart, Vann, Friday, and Koodank rode in the cab of Marn's pickup, while Clem, Gillis, and Skatney rode on top of the heavily loaded vehicle.

Teed watched the two-truck convoy, loaded to the breaking point, slowly crawl away over the rough road. The boy felt a sadness that would stay with him the rest of his life. That was the only home he had known, and when he was finally slapped in the face by raw reality, he had a woe-begone feeling of remorse. He knew that he could never return to that place to live. The mining company would move the dirt to get to the coal as it strip-mined the farm, changing its appearance, leaving an everlasting scar on the land.

Teed was brought back to reality as his father said, "Son, get a chain and tie Ol' Bowser to a porch post and lay a chop sack against the wall for him to lay on. He'll want to go along with us and the cows. I'm afraid he might keep us busy trying to stop him from fighting with other dogs as we go to Blue Domer Creek. I'll send Bart back tomorrow to get him in the pickup truck."

As Teed snapped the chain in place, the dog looked up at him with big, sad eyes. He seemed to sense that his master was leaving without him. Teed did not want to abandon the faithful canine. There was no other alter-native, though. He was faced with the task of helping his father walk the two milk cows to their new home. The dog could create problems along the way, he realized.

The cows stood by the paling fence surrounding the yard, patiently chewing their cuds, as contented as two old Jersey cows could be.

The old house and yard looked empty and forsaken as Teed led Old Horney away. He heard Old Bowser whine as if to ask why he had been left behind.

Teed took one last glance back over his shoulder, just before the house was hidden from view by the stunted white oak trees down near the hog-lot.

Old Bowser was at the end of his chain, wanting to follow. A lonesome howl that started on a low note and faded to nothing followed the drovers through the woods bordering the farm.

That howl was so sad that Teed almost cried. He was leaving many years of wonderful memories behind. Maybe not his entire life of memories, for there were a few years of his life in which he could not remember anything that had occurred—his baby years.

Teed and his father led the cows over hill and dell and across creeks, passing acquaintances on the highway. Many kinfolks and friends waved from cars as they passed, while some greeted the drovers from their porches and yards. Several people waved from fields on the slopes by the road, where they were harvesting late cuttings of hay.

"Them folks should have their crops in already," Marn told Teed as they passed one of Marn's cousins' hay field. Marn knew everyone on the road to Blue Domer Creek and called each by his or her first name.

Teed saw numerous little girls about his age—some younger—some older. As he passed two pretty little girls at play in one yard, that hateful cow he was leading made it a point to stop and do something that was embarrassing for him. He knew that his face was as red as two beets, one stacked on top of the other. What the cow did caused the little girls to squeal and run behind the house, giggling as they fled from sight.

Teed figured for sure that those little twittery girls were laughing at him—not at the cow—and that made his quandary much harder to bear. He assumed that he would be going to school with those girls. The school buses ran from Bass Creek over to Blue Domer Creek and then on to the high school at the county seat at Big Onion Gap. He figured that those girls would recognize him at school and tell others about their seeing him driving a cow along the road. He did not want that to happen.

Teed kicked the cow in his charge. He was so mad that he had to vent his frustrations on something.

Marn put a stop to Teed's shenanigans by saying, "Teed, stop kicking on that cow! We want to have a healthy cow when we get to Blue Domer Creek. A three-legged cow won't be of much benefit to us. She won't be able to stand up on them steep hillsides over there. Just lead her along and don't pay any attention to them little gigglin' girls. You ain't ready to marry one of them right now. You may never see them again."

Even though Marn raked Teed with strong, reprimanding words, there was a twinkle in his eyes and a hint of a smile at the corners of his mouth. He was amused by Teed's actions and his thwarted ego.

"I may never see those little girls again, but I'll see this hateful cow ever' day of my life," Teed complained. He clomped along the road with his cow in tow, mumbling his displeasures to himself.

"If you let a little incident like that bother you as you wage your war with Dan Cupid," Marn said with a loud chuckle, "you have some major hurdles ahead of you that you'll have a hard time jumping."

"That Cupid boy had better stay out of my way if I'm gonna go to war with him!" Teed stormed. "I'm mad enough right now to whup that Cupid feller, this cow—the whole kit and caboodle—bare-handed!"

Marn laughed as he watched Teed stamp his feet and tug at the lead rope tied to the Jersey cow's horns.

*   *   *   *

The drovers reached Blue Domer Creek just as the sun inched its way behind Booger Hill, a tall, hogback-shaped hill, part of the Cumberland Mountain range. The long, hard trip from Coaley Creek had finally ended.

Teed's butt was wiping out his tracks as he trudged his way to the barn.

His father was still going strong, though. Teed was sure that Marn could have carried a cow and drug Teed along with no effort at all.

With the cows safe in the barn, Teed and Marn went to the house, where they found Vann cooking supper.

The rest of the brothers and sisters, Uncle Sprocket, and Cousin Boots were putting the last items of furniture in their permanent places.

Teed was so tired that he lay down on the floor to rest. The new linoleum floor cover felt cool and comfortable and smelled so refreshing. Lying there was so relaxing that he could have gone to sleep, had he not been interrupted by Gillis and Friday running through the house, with Gillis flipping on the light switches and Friday flipping them off.

Marn put a stop to their fun, and Teed was able to lie there and get some much-needed rest. Vann's calling everyone to the big dining room to eat their first meal in the new house roused Teed from his rest.

The meal was sumptuous as always, but Vann apologized to Uncle Sprocket and Cousin Boots for just throwing together a snack.

Uncle Sprocket and Cousin Boots went at the fare put before them and did not complain, nor did the rest of the family.

The greatest excitement with the new surroundings had to be the electric lights. There was no electricity on Coaley Creek, so the bright lights were a new adventure for the children.

There were many comments made about the amount of light that one little light bulb could spread over the big room. That little bulb was many times brighter than the old kerosene lamps used to light the old house.

Teed hoped that he would never have to strain his eyes under the oil lamps again to study and do his homework at night. He figured that he could make straight A's with such bright lights. He would burst his report card wide-open with good grades and make his family proud of him.

After the delicious meal was over, Uncle Sprocket and Cousin Boots thanked Vann for the good food and left for their home on Bass Creek. Everyone watched them drive away in the big coal-hauling truck.

The family then retired to the living room to rest and to talk. There was always a good conversation before bedtime each night. On that particular evening their conversation was about electricity.

"Ain't it interesting how 'lectricity works," Teed remarked, squinting up at the bright light. When he looked at the floor, a black spot in the shape of the light bulb, with a halo-like glow around it, danced before his eyes. That really amazed him. He told Gillis and Friday to try looking at the light bulb and then at the floor like he had done.

"That sure is something," Gillis marveled after squinting at the light and then looking around the room.

"That sure is something," Friday echoed, doing as Teed had suggested.

"Friday, you must never stick a metal object in a 'lectrical outlet such as that plug-in over there," Teed warned, pointing to the opposite wall.

The innocent little girl walked over to the plug-in that Teed had indicated and gave it a thorough inspection. "I won't poke anything in it, Teed," she promised.

"Just make sure that you don't," he said, trying to discourage her from doing such a dangerous thing. "You could get such a surge of 'lectricity that you could get all charged up and get killed, too. 'Lectricity is something that can kill you without you knowing where it comes from, if you don't know anything about it."

"How come you know so much about 'lectric, Teed?" Marn asked.

"Well, Dad, 'lectricity is a very simple thing that is made complicated so people can't understand it and books have to be wrote about it. Then you have to go to school to learn it," Teed said. "Someday I hope to be able to go to a 'lectricity school and learn a lot about it."

"You should go on and study 'lectric so you can work in the mines as a 'lectric repairman," Marn suggested. "I've heard that you can get 'lexey-cuted with juice from a 'lectric wire, if you don't know how to work with it, that is. That's why you should go and study up on it so you can work safe with it. They say that 'lectric workers at the mines make a slop bucket full of money on payday."

"You can get killed dead by it," Teed stated. "It's not dangerous if you know what you're doing. That's why a lot of books have been wrote about it, so that people can learn the right way to work with it 'stead of just jumping in and trying to figure out how it works by experimenting with it."

"You should be a 'lectric engineer," Gillis said. "You already know about all there is to know about that 'lectric stuff."

"I'll have to learn just a little bit more about it before I can become a good engineer," Teed admitted. "I think I can learn the rest of the stuff that I need to know about it in just a few days, that is if I have the chance and have a good teacher to help me when I come to something that I can't figure out by myself."

"We never have had 'lectric before," Marn stated. "So how did you learn so much about it? They don't teach that at Coaley Creek Elementary School, do they?"

"No, they don't teach it there, Dad," Teed grinned. "You have to go somewhere else to study about it. Dump told me about it—about all I need to know. He gave me oral learning. That's learning without any books to go by. He told me with his mouth, and I learned it by listening to him with my ears," Teed told his father.

"Just you be careful when you start learning more about it. Don't be careless and go and get yourself 'lexeycuted 'fore you have a chance to grow up and make a living working with juice," Marn warned. "I know you had to learn about it somewhere—to know all about it like you do."

"I thought maybe that Dump told you with his heel, and you learnt it with your big toe," Gillis said, butting into the conversation, giggling.

"Don't try to be funny when we're talking about 'lectricity," Teed warned Gillis. "Dump told me the right way."

Dump had gone away to study at a big school in Chicago. He had learned the principles of electricity and could do house wiring and radio repairs. He had shared some of that knowledge with Teed.

"Now, Friday," Teed began, "you must remember what I just told you about 'lectrical plug-ins."

"I will, Teed," Friday promised.

Teed could see a look of curiosity on the little girl's face as she continued to run and play.

The conversation about electricity ended. The family was sitting and lying about the room in silence when they heard an awful calamity in an adjoining bedroom.

A scream, followed by a thump on the floor, let everyone know that Friday had experienced something that was painful.

Teed and Gillis bounded up off the floor and scampered to the bedroom to see what had happened to Friday.

"What happened, Friday?" Teed asked, looking at the little girl lying on her back in the middle of the bedroom.

"I poked these bobby pins in that plug-in," she said, wiping tears out of her eyes with the backs of her hands, showing the discomforts from her first experience with electricity. She sniffed loudly and continued, "I wanted to see if you was right about how I could get shocked, Teed. You sure was right!"

"Now, you're all charged up and ready to run," Teed laughed. "Don't do that again, Friday. Promise?"

"Promise," Friday replied.

Teed knew that the little girl was serious and would never poke bobby pins in an electrical outlet again.